Chicago Two Step

A Joseph Hampton Mystery

Jim E. Johnson

Acknowledgements

I want to thank my friends at the Abilene Police Department for answering my questions. Also, I'd like to thank my friend, FBI Agent Michael Edmiston for answering any questions I had.

To Wilma, Mellisa, Mom, Dad, Kathleen and everyone that supports my writing efforts. Also, I'd like to further dedicate this novel to B. Alan Bourgeois of Author's Marketing Guild for providing the publishing tool Ingram Spark.

Forward

Following the Task Force Corpus Christi case of the Little Russian Doll; Corpus Christi Police Captain Pamela Hampton received a call from one of her ace detectives, Sgt. Frank Murphy. Joe and Pam travel to Chicago concerning Murphy's arrest for murder.

What Joe and Pam soon discover; Murphy's arrest provided a cover for a larger mystery revolving around organized crime, human trafficking, and Greek family drama.

Chicago Two Step

Prologue

Danny, Danny it's me Frank! Come on doofus open the door!" The man known as Frank Murphy continued to pound on the door to the apartment belonging to MCPO Daniel Murphy, but no response. He looked around as he found a key to his apartment just above the door on the outside molding. He opened the door to a scene from a horror movie. A neighbor came out due to the disturbance. "Call 911; my brother's dead!"

Moments later, uniformed cops and detectives go into the apartment and confirmed Master Chief Petty Officer Daniel Murphy, his wife Rebecca and son John…were all shot to death. Chicago PD Homicide Det. Ariel Papadakis arrived on the scene. The red-headed Greek detective cousin of CCPD Captain Pamela Hampton took a visual survey of Sgt. Frank Murphy and pulled out her pad. "So, Sgt. Murphy, you told the officer on the scene you just arrived two hours ago at O'Hare Airport, and then took a cab here to your brother's apartment?"

"Yes ma'am; that's exactly what happened."

Ariel nodded and made notes. "According to the neighbor, Mr. Cantu; you were pretty loud out in the hallway; why were you so late getting here?"

"My flight from Corpus Christi experienced mechanical failure and we had to make an emergency landing in St. Louis. We were further delayed for four more hours until a replacement 747 could be prepped for flight; then I arrived, three hours ago as of now. My brother Danny was supposed to pick me up, but I got a text saying his car died on him and he suggested I catch a cab."

"Uh-huh," Ariel said as she looked around and over the six foot tall Irish cop from Texas. The steel in his blue eyes and the matching mix of salt and pepper in his hair told Ariel this cop cooperated with her on every level.

"How was the door to your brother's apartment opened?"

"With this spare key. Danny told me he kept it above the door."

"You see how this looks Sgt. Murphy; you come into town, you allegedly open up the apartment to find your brother lying in a pool of his own blood. How do we know you and your brother don't have a beef and you go all ape shit and kill his entire family?"

Murphy shook his head and laughed, "I came to Chicago to speak with my brother concerning funeral arrangements…our father passed away three days ago in Springfield. I need to call my boss before we go any further."

"Why do that?"

"Because Detective; if you're going to accuse me of murder, I think she needs to hear this in person!"

"Who the hell is your boss Murphy?"

"Corpus Christi Major Case Captain Pamela Papadakis Hampton; I believe she's your cousin…Det. Papadakis?"

Detective Ariel Papadakis let her memo book drop to her side. "Oh shit!"

One

We got off the Lear jet at Chicago's Midway International Airport at the Signature Flight terminal as Pam called in at CCPD. "Hey Jen, we just landed and grabbed our bags. Yes, we're grabbing a rental because until I talk to Murph, I don't know who to trust in this case." Pam's anger matches mine as she continues to speak with our good friend Corpus Christi Police Chief Jennifer Vaughn. "Well, according to Murph, my cousin Ariel placed him under house arrest at his hotel. No, I flew via Signature Flight because I'm here on business and not a family get-together. I don't need my uncles getting involved in this if it's a simple misunderstanding."

"Well I met both Ariel and Nikki at your wedding. Neither seems to be really on the ball unless they speak with your Uncle Sal over at the Intelligence Unit. Tread lightly around your family girlfriend."

"Why do you think I'm having NCIS Asst. Dir. Vale meet us? He and Superintendent Brown are old friends and I can get him to ask why they weren't called in on the murder of a Navy chief and his family." Pam's frustration seems to be subsiding as I check on a rental for our stay in Chicago. As soon as I receive confirmation, Pam ends her call with Jennifer. "They have what we need?"

"No, they're fresh out, but I did give them my cell phone number and I'll get a text when one rental we need comes available." Pam wears her tan business suit with trousers and tan boots as I opt for denim slacks, a plaid long-sleeve shirt and black boots. My attire is out of season for June in the Windy City, but as Pam said this is a business trip; not a social call on the family. But, someone in the family squeals we were coming because Pam's parents wave at us at the other end of the terminal. "How in the hell?"

"Ariel, who else?" Pam's frown deepens as her parents notice and cautiously approach.

"Ma, Pop; what brings you out at this time of day?"

"Joe," Gus said as he looks warily into Pam's eyes. The older man gulps as he gives Pam a wide berth to speak to me. "She's giving us that same look she gave us when Maria tried to get her to retire from law enforcement. Why didn't you call us to tell us you were coming? Why did we have to learn it from my niece Ariel?"

"Did Ariel tell you why Pam and I were coming to Chicago?" I can see in Gus's eyes Ariel left out the 'why' part of our trip to Chicago. "Ariel caught a dead body at the Forest Pointe Apartments where CCPD Det. Sgt. Murphy's brother lived. Murphy found his brother and family murdered a few hours ago. Ariel believed he had something to do with it."

"Well, why is Pam here then if not to see us?"

"Murphy called Pam and told her that Cousin Ariel is holding him as a material witness in the multiple homicides. Here's the problem Ariel's now facing: Murphy's brother was a Navy Chief Petty Officer. And that means, she failed to notify NCIS of the fatality."

"Oh my God," Gus says as he realizes why Pam is so angry and why she didn't tell them of our arrival. "How much trouble is Ariel in at the moment?"

"Considering she didn't notify NCIS of the fatality or that the North Chicago Police Department deferred to the closest District to the base and she caught it as a result; you tell me Gus. How much trouble do you think Ariel is in at the moment?" Gus realizes many people dropped the ball on this fiasco and now my wife is about to blow up like a tactical nuclear war head. There are some days I think my family's bonkers; then we come to Chicago and I realize I don't have it so bad. Pam walks up still angry as her mother stops yelling long enough to let us think. "You find out what happened with Murph?"

"I called Uncle Sal; they moved Murph to the Black Site." Oh man, I heard many horror stories of cops using a secret site for interrogating suspects when time sensitive cases came about.

"I told Sal I wanted him alive and unharmed at the 24th District house in an hour or I was going to call Vale and mobilize Marine Corps SR (Special Response) Teams and head over there with borrowed riot gear!"

Then I get call on my cell from Vale. "Hampton; Leo go!"

I put my phone on speaker, *"Joe, we found the van and we caught two Chicago PD female detectives getting Murphy out of a blacked out van. We've detained Detectives Ariel and Nikki Papadakis. Are these two ladies Pam's cousins?"*

"Leo, it's Pam and unfortunately, yes both are my cousins."

"How would you like me to handle this issue Captain?" I know Leo Vale. He's asking because Pam knows Ariel messed up by not reporting the dead sailor to NCIS. And the trouble is about to brew in a big way.

Pam finally smiles. "Leo my dear friend, order them to take Sgt. Murphy to the District 24 House now and make sure he's suffered no injuries other than his pride and I will consider not pressing charges of false arrest. How you choose to deal with my cousin's lack of good judgment with regards to reporting protocol…you and Chief Superintendent Brown can work that out."

"Fair enough; when can Murphy expect you there?" I look at Pam as Gus and Maria signal, they want us to go with them and delay our intentions on meeting with Murphy. Something is going on and Pam and I are getting tired of this two-step.

"I'll be there in an hour. And Leo, inform my Uncle Rudy over at the FBI Violent Crimes Task Force; his girls are in my doghouse!" Pam hangs up and turns to her mother Maria. "Why are you delaying me from seeing my officer…Mother?"

"You are too angry to do your job correctly! Ariel had every right to arrest that man! He may have murdered his own family. You know how those Irish rogues are Pamela!" Maria spoke out of turn as Pam's fury was just about to blow the roof off of the terminal.

Pam steps past her parents and heads to our rental. I turn and glare at both of them.

"I will try to calm her down enough to convince her to spend some time with you while we're here, but after what Maria just said…you're lucky your daughter doesn't disown you before we leave to go back home."

As I turn to leave, Maria yells, "This is her home Joseph! Why is she doing this to us?" Maria wails and cries as I leave, and I don't look back.

"Mom give you a hard time love?" Pam asks as I reach our nicely optioned 2016 Black Chevy Suburban. I nod as we load up our luggage and get aboard. I let Pam drive since she knows the Windy City better than I do. An hour later, we reach the District 24 House as the van arrives from the black site. Vale smiles and waves as I see Murphy. Apparently, Ariel and Nikki did something, or Murphy wouldn't be sporting a black eye. "Which one of you detectives did this to my sergeant?"

"Prisoners are clumsy in handcuffs Pam!" Nikki said to smart off to Pam. Then her father Captain Rudy Papadakis walked out. "Captain?"

"Tell me you forgot to address Captain Hampton by her rank?" Uncle Rudy steps out of the door as Nikki looks into her father's eyes.

"Come on Pop; it's Pam! What she going to do?" Then he smacks Nikki in the back of the head. "What did I do Pop?"

"You and your sister disrespected one of Pam's detectives. Your sister disrespected him by arresting him for his brother's murder. And I'm betting you gave him the black eye." Murphy smiles and nods the confirmation. Then Uncle Rudy gives Pam her kudos. "Congratulations on your marriage and your promotion Captain Hampton. My apologies for my detectives treating your sergeant in such a brutal manner."

"I appreciate your apology Captain Papadakis; now for the fly in the ointment; how do you plan on making this right?

"Furthermore, what punitive measures will be dealt upon Detective Ariel Papadakis for failure to report the dead Chief Petty Officer named Daniel Murphy as well as his family?"

Before Rudy can stick his foot in his mouth, Leo speaks up, "If I may Captain Papadakis?" Uncle Rudy politely nods. "I am Naval Criminal Investigative Service Assistant Director Leonardo Vale. Detective Ariel Papadakis failed to follow protocol and contact my office at Naval Station Great Lakes concerning the demise of Master Chief Petty Officer Daniel Murphy and his family. As such, Captain Hampton's…question does validate the circumstances?"

Uncle Rudy looks at both his daughters and shakes his head. I have to think he wonders sometimes if the OB-GYN's who delivered these girls, if someone switched his children out with these two models. I watch with bated breath as Rudy walks in front and faces them both. He pulls out his handcuff keys and releases Murphy. "On behalf of the entire fourteen-thousand plus officers and detectives of the Chicago Police Department, I humbly apologize for the treatment you received at the hands of my daughters and fellow cops. Furthermore, we will be handing this case off to NCIS in the spirit of cooperation we would like to continue with all federal law enforcement agencies."

Murphy nodded and offered his hand. "I accept your apology Captain Papadakis. I understand the pressures of the job, the need to resolve a case as quickly as possible; and at times, misunderstandings occur."

Rudy shakes Murphy's hand as Pam hears Murphy's line and walks up next to him. "You really feel that way, or are you being courteous under the circumstances?"

"A little bit of both Skipper," Murphy says as a well-versed veteran cop.

"That's very…generous of you Sgt. Murphy," Uncle Rudy looks at Pam as his shock registers with Ariel and Nikki. "However if I know my daughters, you might want to rethink just how generous you want to be in this situation."

"Pardon me Captain; may I have a word with Det. Murphy over here please?" Uncle Rudy nods to Murphy as he walks over and joins us by the SUV. "First things first; which one gave you the shiner?"

"Your blonde cousin, Nikki I believe is her name?" Pam looks over at Uncle Rudy and nods in Nikki's direction. We watch with amusement as he slaps Nikki in the back of the head again. "You honestly think that method of getting their attention works?"

"There are days it works better than others Frank. Look, I know you already went through the sequence with the trouble twins over there. My thinking; there might be a detail you left out between you left O'Hare to the time you arrived at your brother's apartment."

"Sure thing," Murphy smiles and replays his itinerary from the time he left Corpus Christi to the time he landed at O'Hare and traveled to his brother's apartment at Forest Pointe. The puzzling issue to come from this explanation: what prevented Dan from picking up Frank? Someone had an issue with either Frank, his brother, his family, or someone else entirely different and Frank's family was cast-off. The part that relieves us and Frank Murphy, NCIS has the case and will provide answers. "Dan and I did have one sticking point in all of this; where to bury Dad."

"But that's not serious enough to arrest you for murder, is it?" I ask cautiously of course since I don't know Frank Murphy all that well.

"No, Joe it's not. I…loved my brother Joe…very much!" Then I see this tall, tough Irish cop from Springfield, Illinois, drop to one knee; rest his head on Pam's right shoulder. And my beautiful, short wife tenderly held her most experienced sergeant in her arms and let him cry and mourn his brother's loss.

I watch as my wife comforts her tall Irish sergeant with her own tears of sorrow. "Leo's people will find this hump Frank. They will find him and bring him to justice I promise you." She pats his broad shoulders and steps back a little.

"Okay, get up and let's get you back to your hotel. Captain Papadakis; about the Detectives Papadakis?"

"As much as I'd like to let Sgt. Murphy spank both of these idiots, I call daughters, proper procedure prevents me from doing that. However, I will recommend an Internal Affairs review of this arrest. You two are suspended for fifteen days each, without pay until IAB clears the case."

"Pop you can't!" Ariel starts to protest as Pam glares at her. "It's not right I get punished for doing my job!"

"And that's the cop-out excuse for sloppy detective work!" Pam just received a nod from Uncle Rudy. "That's why some cases take time to develop Ariel. You're only human and you will make mistakes in this job. And on this particular case; you made four: one, you arrested a guy who has an alibi via CCTV footage. Two, you involved your sister in trying to hide him at a black site; three, you failed to involve NCIS due to the death of Master Chief Murphy and four…you called my mother when you found out I was coming here to assess my sergeant's situation. And that fourth point is the one that sticks in my craw the worst! You knew I was coming here and not here to visit my parents and hindered me from getting a clear idea as to why Sgt. Murphy was arrested. If you can't learn to accept the consequences of your actions Ariel, you don't deserve to wear that gold star on your belt!"

"She's right Ariel; you broke the rules to satisfy family ties instead of doing the job right. And as such, I am holding you accountable for those decisions you made." To hear Uncle Rudy say this warms Pam's heart and mine. "Detective Murphy, I assume Asst. Dir. Vale wants you to stick around until your brother's case is resolved?"

"Yes sir he did."

"Then I suggest go get a Chicago dog, take in some music at the House of Blues, go sailing on Lake Michigan, or whatever tourists do when they come to the Windy City. Who knows, between you and Pam; maybe Joe can see the true Chicago others rarely see."

Rudy smiles as Frank Murphy nods in response. "Pam, are you planning on seeing your folks while you're here waiting on NCIS?"

Pam nods…reluctantly, "I'll go to the closest restaurant over by our hotel. I'll call Daddy and let him know which one."

Rudy sends Ariel and Nikki inside the District and walks over to us. "Your mom still won't accept who you are or where you live due to the Duprees?"

"She still thinks…Charlie's family will hurt me or Joe. And she believes in her heart of hearts that unless I have a full home field advantage, I'll get killed where I live and work." Pam's tears begin to fall as she looks away for a moment. "She won't trust me, because of Charlie's brutality. And since she doesn't know Joe all that well, she trusts him even less."

"Do what you have to do," Uncle Rudy smiles. Did I mention I like him?

Two

We check into the City Suites Chicago Hotel on West Belmont Street. And I discover right down the street is a Papa Papadakis' restaurant from the hotel. Although evening set in, the hour is still early enough to enjoy a fantastic meal. Pam and I invite Murphy along so he wouldn't be stuck in his hotel room waiting on delivery pizza. Besides, I called Gus earlier after Pam informed her family we would dine at that location.

He agreed with me Sgt. Murphy should enjoy some Chicago hospitality on Pam's family at the closest restaurant location. As we walk in the front door, Pam's older sister Athena greets us. She stands three inches taller than Pam and also shares Pam's chocolate brown eyes with a straight, almost 1960's flower child hairstyle. Athena is called Thea by her nieces and nephews as well as her family; I guess it's just easier that way. "Pam; my little sister is back so soon!" Both embrace and then Thea hugs me. "And you brought the handsome Longhorn with you; how are you Joe?" Athena's a lovely sister-in-law, but I always wonder how she ended up married to an Irish lawyer named Michael Flynn. I guess the version of *My Big Fat Greek Wedding* exists only in the movies.

I look around the restaurant and ask, "Where's Mike at Thea?"

Thea rolls her eyes due to the Greek/Irish drama in Mike's family. "His mother fell, and she still insists after all these years, I'm still trying to poison my husband!"

"I thought Mike loved Greek food?" Pam asks as she gives Thea her playful eye.

"He does sis I just started fixing some staple Irish meals as well. Anyway, as you can see drama queens exist in all families," Thea smiles as she meets Murphy. "And you must be Sgt. Murphy; I'm Thea Flynn, pleased to meet you."

"I'm pleased to meet you as well ma'am. Please, call me Frank." Murphy smiles as Thea nods. However, a ruckus from the back moves forward as Maria's brother, Det. Sgt. Sal Constantine walks up with his less than intelligent son, Cook County District Attorney Angelo Constantine. "Who is that Pam?"

"Ah, Pam…good to have you home…for a visit," Uncle Sal says as he hugs Pam warmly; then me. "Joe, what brings you up here with Pam?"

"Sgt. Murphy, meet Intelligence Unit Command Sgt. Salvatore Constantine, my maternal uncle and this is son, Cook County Assistant District Attorney Angelo Constantine." Pam's lack of mercy toward Angelo centers on the fact he kept groping Pam at our wedding. Other than Pam, Angelo fears me more than his own family. "You see Frank; I have a rather ambitious cousin in the District Attorney's office. So ambitious in fact, I learned he tried to refile the murder charge against you." Every family member turns to glare at Angelo. Pam begins her inquisition. "What new evidence came to light to warrant refiling the murder charge…Counselor?"

What strikes me as profound is Thea walks up and joins Pam in the grilling. Gotta love Greek family drama! "And as a follow up…Counselor, and I use that term ever so loosely; what new witnesses or confirmations have come forward to waste taxpayer's time and money to refile said charge against Sgt. Murphy?" Murphy looks at Thea as she presents him with a card. "I'm a criminal defense attorney as well as a civil trial attorney and I have a credential in all fifty states, including Texas."

Murphy and I smile at the same time as Angelo tugs at his shirt collar and realizes whatever con he's tried to perpetrate; just sank to the bottom of Lake Michigan. He laughs nervously as Pam hands me her badge and her off-duty Beretta Pico nine millimeter pistol. She walks up and punches Angelo square in the kisser. The family, Sal included, stand in total shock due to Pam's rage. Maria walks up and screams, "What is wrong with you?

"You bring that—that criminal into my restaurant; you assault your cousin in my restaurant. Who do you think you are?"

Pam stares blankly into her mother's angry eyes. Maria pushed all the right buttons to the point; Pam became violent with her cousin Angelo. She manipulated the whole scene to where Pam was the villain of this macabre drama. So Pam's only recourse now is to do the unthinkable. "No one...you care to know...ever again...Mrs. Papadakis. Since you refuse to let me be my own person except who you think I should be and refuse to allow me the courtesy to do my job as I see fit; I am no one you care to know. From here on out, I am...*xeno* to you." From the pronounced shock inside the family and restaurant, Pam just disowned her family. And from what Dad told me once, it's an uncommon occurrence, but it does happen from time to time.

Gus walks up quickly and whispers; "Think about what you're doing and saying! Do you have any, any idea what you're about to do?"

"Yes sir I do...do you...Mr. Papadakis? Do you know what I'm about to do and more importantly, do you understand why?" Pam looks pleadingly into Gus's eyes for any kind of recognition as to her plan. Tears roll down the old man's face as he nods and quickly kisses Pam on both cheeks. He tearfully walks away as she faces Maria's confused look. "Since, Madam, you cannot accept me for who I am and whom I choose to be...I am *xeno* to you; motherless, childless; no family in Greece to speak of from this day forward. The moment you spurned me to anger for your own selfish desires, is the day I died to you!" She rips off the metallic heirloom cross her grandmother Constantine gave to her as a teenager, throws it to the ground and turns her back to her mother. Pam looks to me and smiles. "Let's get out of here."

"We're with you...Skipper!" I said as I glare unyielding at Maria. Murphy and I follow Pam out of the restaurant and get into our SUV. I call Vale. "Hey Leo."

"Joe, if you're calling me, something's terribly wrong."

"Pam…just declared she was…a barbarian to her own family," and I can't believe I just said that to Leo. "It appears I am her only family now. And we might need to bring Murphy to your office at Naval Station Great Lakes."

The silence on the other end sounds deafening since the Leo Vale I know is never at a loss for words. *"I hope you know that will make things more challenging with Pam on the outs with her family. Joe, is there any way to salvage the relationships at this point?"*

"Pam's mom Maria pushed this little rebellion of Pam's heart against her family. The ball's in Maria's court now old buddy."

"Do Jennifer and Jason need to come up here? Something tells me Jen's itching for more news concerning Murphy's situation."

"I'll get Pam to send her a Skype call later on tonight. Maybe if Jason's around we can put our heads together and help you figure out who killed Murph's family and see who in Chicago PD wanted Pam home to shadow this thing." Pam gives me a sideways glance as she keeps her eye on the road. "Look Leo, I know I sound like I'm grasping at straws, but someone in Pam's family wanted her home besides Maria." And I even hate to say this while Pam's driving, but I'm thinking these two issues are somehow connected."

"I hate to say it Leo, but I think Joe's right. My mother allowed me to disown her; that means something's rotten in Chi-town!"

Leo Vale now understands why Pam did what she did and why Gus didn't put up a fight. And now I understand; the only other place Pam had little influence other than New Orleans was Chicago. As the scripture goes, *only in his own hometown is a prophet without honor.* And that means because Pam was technically the prodigal daughter, someone felt that weakness must be exploited. "Leo, I think this little issue has roots back in Corpus Christi. Someone killed Murphy's family and tried to set him up to take the fall. Let's talk turkey with Jen and Jace from your office OPS area Leo."

"Are you all three staying at City Suites Chicago?"

"Yes, why do you ask?"

Again with the deafening silence; I swear talking to Leo Vale somedays is like talking to Jason on the phone. Must be a SEAL thing. Anyway I hear lots of talking and rummaging around in the background. *"I'm sending a team over to meet you three. Go upstairs and get your stuff then come back down. Special Agent Scott Lassiter will meet you at the front desk when you return to the lobby. Drop your rental off at the closest rental agency you dealt with and get on station ASAP. You copy?"*

"Copy that Asst. Dir. Vale!" I hang up as we arrive at City Suites. We go upstairs and get our bags and any personal affects we left earlier. By the time we hit the lobby, we are met by someone not of the federal agent variety. A short dark-haired woman with piercing blue eyes approached. "Yes ma'am?"

"I am Tatyana Brezhnev–Russian Federal Security Bureau; we are ordered to escort you to Naval Station Great Lakes to deal with the murder of one Master Chief Petty Officer Daniel Murphy." Funny, Leo never mentioned Russian FSB working with him on this case. I wonder if this has something to do with the Petrov case. "Mr. Hampton, is something wrong?"

"How did you know my name is Hampton Ms. Brezhnev?" I slowly pulled my Sig-Sauer P-226 nine millimeter pistol from my pancake holster and pointed at FSB Agent Brezhnev. "I will not ask again Agent Brezhnev, how did you know my name was Hampton?"

Then behind them a tall younger man yells, "Federal agents, drop your weapons now!" Brezhnev and her agents drop their weapons as I put mine on the ground. Former NCIS Special Agent Hampton, CCPD Captain Hampton and CCPD Sgt. Murphy?" We all nod as the young man smiles. His agents cuff Brezhnev and her brood as he says, "NCIS Special Agent Scott Lassiter; pleased to meet you folks."

I smile and shake the young man's hand. "We're pleased to meet you as well Agent Lassiter!"

Three

After Lassiter and I drop my rental off at the closest Avis Rental terminal, we drive over to the Great Lakes Field Office of NCIS. "Agent Lassiter...?"

"Scott, or Scotty; Jason Vaughn told me you actually hate formality. So I hope it's okay to call you Joe?" Lassiter asks with a great deal of respect. I shake his hand and nod. "I never thought I'd meet one of Jason's contemporaries from Desert Storm and Bosnia."

"Yeah we snipers are an unusual breed Scotty. We can work as teams or alone and still accomplish the mission. The funny part is sometimes a Marine Corps sniper scout can team up with Navy SEAL sniper ten years after Desert Storm and teach future Iraqi cops how to be good cops."

I see Lassiter smile as we drive through the NS Great Lakes main gate. He shows the Shore Police guard his ID and he waves us on through. "Yeah: Crime Scene Processing in a desert environment; Forensic Evidence Collection procedures, criminal profiling, and...Humane Interrogation techniques. Jason accused you of being a real character."

"Me; that West Texas Rattlesnake; I'm gonna slap him behind his head so hard; his grandchildren will feel the pain! What a jerk!" I look at Lassiter after my playful rant and both of us laugh. "Actually, we both tried to get each other in trouble a bit during those early days of the Iraqi Police Academy. But we had lots of fun either in war time or peace time for us."

"Sounds like my boss and I back three years ago during the Gulf Coast Wraith case; I learned a lot working with that in-house task force. I also learned to have a love/hate relationship with the CIA. I wanted to kill that son of a bitch Callaway."

"Wished I could have been there Joe; I'd loved to have seen that bastard's face when Jason nailed him."

I could hear the desire to take out a guy like Callaway in Pam's voice.

"Scotty let me put it to you this way: Jason fought Callaway like a Samurai warrior and made sure Callaway would never live to hurt another soul. Your friend Hiro Sakura…taught him well." We park the vehicle and walk into the office front door and then take the escalator up to the second floor. When the elevator we take stops on the fourth floor, Pam and Murphy meet us outside the Navy Yard's twin of the Multiple Threat Analysis Center or MTAC.

Vale meets us as Lassiter, and he have a short and quiet exchange. Vale turns to us. "Ladies and gentlemen, let's adjourn inside MTAC please?"

Moments later we enter MTAC to a similar setup with stadium seating and what appears to be an IMAX screen with lots of smaller images. Members of Leo's analytical staff keep tabs on possible threats coming from across the Great Lakes from Canada. As we all get seated, he calls on his phone and the doors to MTAC open again. Pam and I, as well as Murphy stare in shock as CCPD Police Chief Jennifer Vaughn and Task Force Corpus Christi under the command of NCIS SAC Jason Vaughn; stand before us. "As you can see Captain Hampton; this situation is more serious than you imagined."

"So it would seem Asst. Dir. Vale; so I am to assume Sgt. Murphy's continued problems with my CPD family members, revolves around the Krontzky family's efforts to locate the Little Russian Doll?" Pam asks knowing the answer already.

Jennifer turns and uses a clicker to survey several crime scenes since her sister Katerina disappeared with her parents, Gerald, and Grace Moran. "Each of the crime scenes represents a family member of officers from CCPD as well as CPD. The perps in Corpus Christi all have ties to the Krontzky Crime family of Siberia. The Siberian mobsters are seeking this woman," Jennifer put up Katerina's picture on the big screen. "Her name is Katerina Svetlana Petrov; Miss Petrov…is my half-sister.

"Back in March, I hired Hampton Investigations to provide security for Katerina as well as my parents."

Jason takes over, "When DMD International stepped in to assist the Russian government in an effort to locate Miss Petrov, the company was unwittingly duped into the Krontzky family by one of their enforcers; a Russian FSB Colonel Anatoly Nikola Kirov. A financial arrangement was struck between us and the Krontzky family to allow Katerina unencumbered immigration freedom to become a US citizen. Kirov tried to kill Katerina and her mother. He died for his efforts."

Jennifer completes the briefing, "My parents and Katerina decided to go off the grid until it was determined her safety was of no concern. The Krontzky family reneged on the deal. That's why all these cops' families were killed. Pam, your families are so big; they can't possibly kill everyone. So they did the next best thing: they separated you from your root family. And that's why FSB Agent Brezhnev appeared at your hotel; she works for Krontzky."

Pam rises from her seat and slowly walks up to Jennifer. Jennifer removes her tan blazer and stands her ground as Pam pulls back and lands a haymaker punch on Jennifer's right jaw. "Pam, what are you doing?" ATF Special Agent Leah McCoy cries out.

When everyone descends to restrain Pam, Jennifer yells, "No! I caused this problem; I need to atone for it! Pam, Maria called me a few minutes ago and told me what you did. She told me…pushing you to do what you did, protects you more than the rest of the family."

Red-haired Leah with her green blouse and blue jeans with black boots comforts Jennifer as the Nubian goddess of the TFCC-FBI desk Cass Coltrane comes over to comfort Pam. Cass's white blouse and navy slacks, moves with her in her red peep-toed sandals and she takes Pam into her arms. "Back in Corpus, I know why we were left out of the big picture. Pam, regardless of how these monsters treated Jen, when they come after one of us, they jump on all of us.

"That includes you girlfriend. So, we added one more person to this little coalition of agents, cops and Marines!"

I smile from ear-to-ear when a short Marine Corps officer appears in civilian attire. Marine Corps Captain Laquita Boggs came from behind Cass and opened her arms wide. "Hey Girl; where's the party?" Pam simply walks up and bear hugs Quid as we call her. Then Quid gently grabs Pam's face and holds it in her soft hands. "Jessup sends his regards. I told him what you and Murph did during my case to get me back from hell. So he tells me to call Vale and ask if TFCC needs a Devil Dog to ride shotgun on this adventure. When Vale gives us the go ahead, Jessup tells me go help our Marines and that's an order!"

Pam looks deeply into Quid's mischievous eyes, "Seriously?"

"What, you doubt me girlfriend?" Quid looks at me and winks. I shake my head as she resumes, "Now Pammy Pam; would ole' Quid feed you a line…of bull?" And when she grins at my wife, Pam shakes her head at that point.

"Oh no Quid; you'd never, ever feed me a line of bull. But you might…bullshit me!" Pam smiles as does Quid and everyone in MTAC roars with laughter. Now, Pam and I know what's going on and what we need to do. The question now is…how? "Okay, okay…everyone who helped Jen protect Kat is here. And Kat's case is related to Murph's troubles and mine. We need intel; as much of it as we can get. Until we have an idea of how far spread Krontzky reach is here, I'm not approaching any of the thirty-seven hundred cops I'm related to. They're being watched from more than one location, so we have multiple enemies in multiple areas. So, I need the help of those who can get it and let my family know; it's being handled."

Vale nods as NCIS Special Agent Darius Coltrane steps up. "I agree Leo. We, you and I as well as Cass and Quid can accomplish the intel-gathering part." Everyone mostly wears jeans in some sort of fashion with tasteful top or shirt with boots of different varieties.

"Special Agent Sean "Lightning" McCoy sits at a computer console station tickles computer keys across two keyboards. "Lightning, how close are we to getting up?"

"Almost there," Lightning says as he turns to Pam. "Someone else besides Jen…owes you an apology Pam." The screen lights up with the image of a woman who heads up one of the most powerful, influential corporations on earth. She and her husband both appear on the screen wearing navy blazers and white tops. Pam looks intently into the somber expressions of the Prince and Princess of Clan Terru; Dr. and Mrs. David Matthews.

"Well, I was wondering when I'd hear from you two. I figured the moment Jen realized I disowned my family, and why…I'd be getting some message from Dallas." Pam continues to look into those somber expressions, and she concludes something's happened. "I know the Krontzky have reneged. And I know part of that decision resulted in the Morans going off the grid with Katerina. They think I know where she is, don't they?"

David sighs heavily as he responds to Pam's question, *"I spoke with Alexander yesterday his time. Apparently, Grigori Krontzky planned on reneging the moment Alexander paid his debts off. Alexander's response was to cut the messenger's hands off and put € 2,000 euros in each hand. Then sent the man back to Krontzky as sushi. Pam, we are grieved by them subjecting your family to this nonsense. And Jen, we should have found another way other than Jason going to all that expense!"*

"For my part, I can forgive you." Pam smiles. "Jen, not my place!"

Dominique nods, *"After all you suffered Pamela, your generosity to this point is unfathomable and…much appreciated. Jennifer; how do I make this right between us? You were right and I was wrong. And I caused Jason to find a solution I was…too cowardly to reach myself. I…regret causing that difficulty."*

"If and when the time comes, Madame Matthews; we'll find a secluded spot where I can give the ass-kicking you so richly deserve!" Jennifer speaks like a Marine Corps Drill Instructor. And when I see Dominique nod, she knows that time between them will occur, but not now. "The main concern we have now is the lack of intelligence with the Krontzky family quietly terrorizing the Papadakis and Constantine families. Pam asked some folks to go out into Chicago and see what can be ascertained. In lieu of that ass-kicking I owe you Nikki, would you be able to…assist with that difficulty?"

I could see Dominique smile that feral grin of hers when she wanted something or could help for something in return. *"I…might be able to help, for a price!"* I watch as David hides his eyes while shaking his head. He looks to Dominique who gives him a sigh of frustration, *"Oh all right; Grigori has a son Alexi who frequents the Red Square Spa. And he owns a residence off of Winchester."*

"You saved yourself that ass-kicking Nikki old girl," Jennifer smiles her own feral grin; the same grin she smiled the night she and Dominique almost had a knock-down drag out brawl on a beach in Port Aransas, Texas. "We appreciate the intel as well."

"What do you plan on doing?" David's question isn't out of line, but the timing of his query makes me wonder…why?

Pam answers the question; and even I'm stunned by her response. "While others discover how wide-spread this infection of the Krontzky goes as far as the danger to my thirty-seven hundred relatives, I'm paying a visit to Alexi Krontzky. And I won't be going alone. However until I speak with members of the allegedly threatened parties, I will wait a day or two. Unless of course, DMD Security…refuses the Krontzky family leeway in any shape or form."

This time David smiles the feral grin. *"I already spoken with the Clan Elders; every member whether human or not, has washed their hands of the Krontzky family. We informed Siberia no more extensions or considerations.*

"The moment they came after the people who assisted with Katerina's escape, is the moment the entire world turned on them. My elders informed me, how I handle this issue, is my own affair; they will support my decision."

Pam's smile brightens the MTAC area and Jennifer sees her Major Case Command Officer just seen the light break through the clouds. "David, when and how you wish to deal with Grigori; is your business. I might start a Chi-town rumble on Alexi since my mother's this terrified!"

"Oh lord, don't want to be in Chicago when that rumble goes down," Dominique quips as even Jennifer chuckles at the prospect of Pamela Hampton declaring war on the Chicago Krontzky family. *"I saw that Chief Vaughn...you laughed!"*

"Still, I agree with Captain Hampton; she needs to talk to the elders of the Papadakis/Constantine families to see how wide-spread the Krontzky's have gotten in Chicago." Both look at one another as Jennifer continues, "And if she'll have me, I'd be honored to go along. And I know this is her lead."

Pam looks into Jennifer's eyes and sees the genuine sorrow from the incident. If Pam takes Jennifer along, Jason and I can tag along in case some idiot from the Krontzky family tries something funny. Pam walks back up to Jennifer and Pam's eyes tear up. "I'm...sorry for punching you in the jaw."

Jennifer sighs and hugs Pam. "I'll remind you when I sucker-punch you during hand-to-hand combat requalification." Pam gulps as Jennifer smiles. "You want me to go with you?"

"Yeah, I do; we'll take our hubbies along in case we get mugged. A couple of Spec-Ops guys to protect us would make the average street punks rethink causing us trouble." Jason and I nod and smile as we look around the crowd. "The rest of you who know Chicago, divvy up the city and districts and see who knows what. Frank, I need you to hang here with Lightning."

"You got it Skipper," Murphy agrees since Angelo tried to re-file a bogus murder charge on him.

Leo hands out assignments and orders pizza for those who need food as Pam, the Vaughns and I, drive back to the same location of Papa Papadakis' Restaurant over on West Belmont. Jennifer looks over the sheet Leo handed her. "How warm of a reception should we expect, knowing you're on the outs with your family Pam?"

"I wished I knew Jen. Ma's really upset, and I feel as if I'm working three cases at once; yours with the Russians, mine with Murph's troubles, and whatever Ma's hiding. And that last part I fear is the lynch-pin to this whole visit!"

Four

When we arrive at the restaurant, to our surprise, Gus is posing as a maître d at the host desk. "Good evening folks, welcome to Papa Papadakis' Restaurant; a table for four?"

"Yes, please kind sir?" Jason asks politely as he uses British vernacular like a well-seasoned gentleman of the realm. I knew those years being Lady Cecilia's stepson taught him some refinement. Of course four years at the Naval Academy at Annapolis didn't hurt either!

Gus seats us as, of all people, Ariel serves as our waitress. She frowns down at Pam as I look to Gus. "The ladies will have iced tea and Mr. Vaughn and I will have water please…Nikki's your name?"

"No sir, I'm Ariel; but I have a younger sister name Nikki," Ariel smiles. Finally, I get a smile due to all the drama earlier in the day. "My apologies, I've had a rough day. Would you prefer a stronger cocktail prior to dinner?"

Jennifer nods to everyone, "I might want a glass of red Merlot as well as my husband please?"

"My wife and I will have a non-alcoholic beer please?" I ask Ariel. She nods and goes to get our cocktails. "Let's see what's good tonight?"

As we look over our menu, Pam starts, for her, a sensitive conversation. "You know Jen; I lied to myself about why I came here."

"Why do you think that Pam? Your purpose was to come here and figure out why Murph was getting railroaded right?" When Pam begins to fidget, I get nervous; because it means she meant to discuss something with me important, and she forgot. "Pam, why didn't you want to see your parents when you landed?"

Then I see the tears glistening in Pam's eyes. She's about to flood the restaurant.

I'm not kidding one bit. You ever see a Greek woman cry when they are extremely upset? Let me tell you buddy, it's not pretty! "Jen, I went to see your OB-GYN Dr. Tanaka; about that second opinion?"

Apparently, Jennifer and Pam spend time discussing those issues pertaining to women and having children. I know Pam's OB-GYN told Pam her uterus was too damaged by her years of marriage to Dupree, to safely carry a baby to term. So, she went to Jen's doctor…Amy Tanaka, and her specialty was difficult challenges in carrying babies to term. Jennifer nods. "About you being able to carry a baby to term; what did she say?" Pam's tears flow and she violently shakes her head. Jennifer gasps, "Oh my god; I'm so sorry Pam!" Jennifer reaches over and embraces Pam as she continues to cry. I prayed, oh how I prayed for a different outcome, even with Dr. Tanaka's opinion.

I take over from Jen hugging Pam and her cries intensify. So much it catches Maria's attention. She comes over and starts her taunts, "What is wrong with this woman? Is the food not to her liking?"

Jason rescues the moment, "Excuse me ma'am, are you the head waitress or hostess for this establishment?"

"No, I co-own the restaurant chain with my husband. Why is the lady crying; is it due to a guilty conscience, or the fact God cursed her somehow?" That did it! I rise from my seat about to express my blind outrage when Pam leaps out of her chair and runs to the lady's room. Jennifer nods and goes after her. "Oh, I must've hit a nerve!"

"Aunt Maria?" Ariel asks as she approaches. "I'm sorry Mr. Hampton?" I nod to Ariel. "I partially overheard the conversation as I was bringing you your pre-dinner cocktails. I'm very sorry for the upsetting news sir."

"Ariel, your…sensitivity to my wife's…discomfort is commendable. Allow me?" Ariel nods as I hand her a fifty dollar bill. "I hope that will help you in your time of need?"

"It will; thank you Mr. Hampton.

"Would you like to order for your wives, or do you prefer to wait until they return?"

Jason and I nod to one another. "I prefer to wait until our wives return Ariel. Mine may not want to stay for the meal…due to Mrs. Papadakis' rude reception." As I say that, Gus walks up and the fury in his eyes makes me want to pull Jason under the table and batten down the hatches!

Gus simply looks at Maria's terror-filled eyes and points to the kitchen. Maria gulps and solemnly walks back to the kitchen. "I'm sorry to hear that."

"That your wife upset mine Mr. Papadakis?" I ask pointedly. Something tells me Gus knows why Maria's acting like this nightmare I've never seen before. And the scary part, we only landed in Chicago this morning!

Gus's fury subsides as he calms down. "Pardon me for the outburst gentlemen. Normally my wife is the paragon of generosity and gentle manners, but she received a mysterious letter two weeks ago."

Jason takes the lead and I love how he gets people to talk. I wished I developed that talent when I was still NCIS. "Pardon me for asking, Mr. Papadakis, was the nature of the letter…threatening in any manner? I ask because I'm a federal agent and a criminal profiler. I could tell you if you have a legitimate threat or a cruel practical joker."

"I'm not sure; my wife won't talk about it." I was afraid Gus would say that. Jason and I look at one another and realize Alexi Krontzky threatened Pam's mother…possibly about Pam. "But if she happens to have the note on her, what would you like me to do?"

"You have a brother-in-law on the job?" I ask and Gus nods. "I suggest should you procure the note, take it to him. Or better yet, call me." I hand Gus an updated business card. "Agent Vaughn and I might be in a better position to help in ways, you can't imagine."

"That would be a miracle for sure," Gus smiles as Jennifer and Pam return.

Pam's eyes were dry, and it seems she repaired her makeup. "Welcome back ladies and I apologize for my wife's treatment of you…is it Captain Hampton?"

"It is Mr. Papadakis and I'm sorry for causing a scene earlier." Pam's gracious demeanor she inherited from Gus…apparently! "I received some…upsetting news from my…OB-GYN. I went to another for a second opinion, and the same report was given…concerning my uterus."

Gus understood what Pam said. Pam just told Gus she can't have children. Gus's eyes well up with tears and he embraces Pam; to share in her agony. "I am so, so, sorry…Pamela. I wish I could help you through this…tragedy."

Pam smiles through her teary eyes. At least one member of her family…still loves her in her eyes, "I wish you could too…Pop." Pam looks up into Gus's eyes and he continues to cry. "I know about the letter she received from Alexi Krontzky. You never knew the name, I found out a couple of hours ago. And I know he setup a Chicago office for his family business at the Red Square Spa. I'm going over there tomorrow and pick a fight like Nikki would."

Gus looks back as Ariel approaches to take our order. "I thought she picks all the fights?" Pam couldn't stop herself from laughing at Gus's joke. Even Ariel chuckles a little at the light-hearted accusation.

Ariel gets in on the Greek comedy routine. "No Uncle Gus; Nikki picks the fights, I just goof up and can't figure out how I can be a better cop."

"Try taking an online course or go take classes in crime scene management," Pam smiles. She nods Ariel to come over to the table. "Let's get four lamb kabobs, traditional Greek salad, and four pieces of Apple Milopita. You get that Ariel?"

"I'll have it out in a bit." Ariel smiles as she goes to the kitchen to place our order.

Gus allows Pam to sit down and relax, "Since Maria was so rude; you can have your meal and drinks on the house."

"That's very kind of you Mr. Papadakis," Jason smiles. "Sir, this would be a good time to see if you can…procure that alleged letter?" Gus smiles and goes back to his office as we enjoy our pre-dinner cocktails. "You know, I love the décor of the dining room Pam. Who came up with this scheme?"

"Ma did," I could see the pride in Pam's eyes as she tells Jason about her family's business model. "When Ma and Pop started this chain, they felt one decorating scheme with one tasty menu would bring in the crowds, and they weren't wrong. Even after thirty years, you want Greek food a family can afford; you come to a Papa Papadakis restaurant." Fifteen minutes pass as Ariel receives assistance from her sister Nikki and brings out our salads and main course. "Thank you, ladies, it looks delish!"

"You're welcome," Nikki says as she bends down, "I hear from a certain member of my family you plan on picking a fight tomorrow at the Red Square Spa. Anyone we're interested in over at Pop's house?"

Jennifer smiles at Nikki, "Alexi Krontzky; he a person of interest with your father's task force?"

"Oh yeah; but wire-taps at Red Square Spa indicate he's keeping it all above board. You won't get this guy to flip on anyone without working at it Pam," then Nikki sighs, "Excuse me, Captain Hampton."

"It's…okay…Nikki; a familiarity in this situation is acceptable. Besides, as far as family is concerned, I think only you, your sister and Pop even care about my concerns. The rest of the family will, in time; but I don't have time to make nice with Mrs. Maria Papadakis." After Pam makes her blistering statement, Maria comes from the back. "Madam?"

Maria gives us a matron-like look as she faces four seated patrons. She looks away and then back to us. "My husband has…informed me, you are receiving your meal for free due to my rudeness earlier."

"That's correct Mrs. Papadakis," Jason responds so Pam can remain silent and not cause another scene. "However, my immediate supervisor can be…persuaded to reimburse your husband for our meal, provided you assist us with an evidentiary matter."

"What sort of…evidentiary matter sir?" Maria asks as she glares at Pam and Pam pays no attention to her.

"It has come to our attention, that Alexi Krontzky of the Grigori Krontzky Crime Family of Strelka, Siberia; sent you a letter threatening the safety of your daughter who is a cop and the other thirty-seven hundred Greek cops related to you." Jason lets that little fact settle on Maria's conscience. "Now, if you so choose to invoke your rights, I can obtain a federal search warrant which will serve tomorrow morning. But by the time we get a federal magistrate to sign off on a warrant, Mr. Krontzky could conceivably kill eighteen-hundred members of your family wearing stars. I'd like to prevent that at all cost."

"What about Sgt. Murphy…the Irish scum?" Maria asks as she continues to glare down at Pam. Now she's raising the ire of a Comanche half-breed Navy SEAL. The part Maria fails to understand; when Jason gets angry, he doesn't yell, he thinks like a general on a battlefield.

"Very well; excuse me Mr. Papadakis?" Jason calls over to Gus. "Apparently my methods of gentle persuasion in obtaining the letter threatening your family, have ended in a case of Sgt. Murphy's situation being mentioned…again for a tiresome fourth time. And since the letter may possibly aide in the protection of multiple members of your family sir, I have no choice but to serve a unilateral federal search warrant on all your restaurants, personal as well as corporate vehicles, even your home and all buildings attached to your business interests sir."

Gus glares at Maria and shakes his head. Again, he has the fury in his eyes I fear could make Medusa turn to stone. "I will not let him destroy everything I've worked hard to build for your damned, foolish, and arrogant pride! Captain Hampton?"

Pam nods as Gus speaks, "Would you accompany my wife along with both of my nieces to our offices here and obtain your evidence? And if she refuses to cooperate; arrest her on…federal obstruction charges…I believe that's correct Agent Vaughn?" Jason nods as Maria sinks into a nearby chair. "Well woman, will you do as I say?"

"I will…husband," Maria says solemnly as she glares at Pam. Pam's neutral expression makes Ariel and Nikki shake their heads at their aunt's continual stubbornness. Before they get too far, Maria turns to face Pam. "Why, why can't you allow your cousin Angelo to do his job?"

"You still consider me family; after the way you continue to treat me like a barbarian?" Maria's stoic glare continues, "Fine, Sgt. Murphy is being held at NS Great Lakes as a material witness in an NCIS investigation into the death of his brother Master Chief Petty Officer Daniel Murphy and Chief Murphy's family. As such, by federal law, the Cook County District Attorney's office can only provide information or file for jurisdiction. I would think after all the shop talk you've been exposed to Madam, you would understand the procedures and why they exist." Pam lets that little bit of knowledge settle on Maria's pointed little matriarchal head. "Now that we've dallied long enough, may we get that letter before my handcuffs leap out of their resting place and onto your lovely wrists Mrs. Papadakis, please?"

Maria nods as she, Pam and the girls disappear into the back. Gus walks up and shakes Jason's hand. "Thank you for helping me out with a stubborn wife. Maria feels she has to protect the kids fiercely; even when she thinks such protection is more beneficial than the alternative." Moments later all four women return with Pam holding up a number ten white envelope. "You found it?"

"It was in Aunt Maria's purse," Ariel takes a breath and continues, "However; Aunt Maria continues to be…aggravating by contacting Thea as to the…manner of your request Agent Vaughn."

Jason chuckles and shakes his head. "Not a problem Ariel, I'm sure we can explain the general scope of this request when Thea arrives."

Five

Thea walks in wearing jeans, a royal blue t-shirt and tan sandals. "Okay, Mike calmed the kids down before I came over here. What's going on gang?"

"They are violating my civil rights!" Maria cries out, "This barbaric police captain stole a letter sent to me! I want it back!" I watch as Thea shakes her head and she realizes Maria's overreacting for drama purposes. I nod as Thea nods back. She knows her mother's attitude stems from the contents of the letter.

"Before I decide whether or not your case holds any water, Mrs. Papadakis, may I see the letter please Captain Hampton?" Pam hands Thea the letter and after viewing its contents, she hands it back…to Pam. "You call me in the middle of the night, to come here and wrestle a threatening letter out of the hands of authorities because you're being petty…Mother?" Maria gives Thea a look of *so what?* Thea shakes her head and turns to Pam. "You need that letter worse than my mother."

Pam sighs as we all turn to leave. Maria yells, "So all my female children abandon me! Serves me right to have had ungrateful daughters!" We receive to go boxes as Thea turns to respond in anger to Maria.

Pam stops her. "No Thea; that's what she wants. She wants a reason to complain so everyone will feel sorry for her. Come on; we'll drop your car off and tell Mike we'll take you out for a drink and explain the whole story. I have some…things I need to tell you anyway."

I ride with Pam and Thea as we head over to Thea's apartment over on West Adams Street! Once we get reacquainted with Mike and Thea's boys, Liam, and Sean, we meet Jason and Jennifer over at Spectrum Bar and Grill on South Halsted.

"Okay, what's gotten Mom's goat…so to speak?"

Pam smiles sadly, "As you can see by what you read in that letter; unless the Krontzky family gets the location of Katerina Petrov by close of business hours tomorrow, they will bring in muscle from out of town and slaughter our entire family. And here's the cruel part: no one at this table snacking and drinking with you, knows Miss Petrov's location."

"I think what Maria tried to do is hold Murph over our heads as a way to glean Katerina's location from us; but we don't know," I accent that note because Jennifer's parents left no trail to speak of to follow. "Murph is being held as a material witness to his family's deaths."

"And unless Ma's willing to trust the law enforcement branch of our family, she's allowing these Russian Cossacks to intimidate her into rolling over and dying without a fight…unbelievable!" We could all see Thea's mind racing due to the near dangerous experience Maria's trying to cause. "Now that you have the letter, what's next?"

Pam smiles her impish grin; I sort of love that one. "I'm having Ariel and Nikki put the word out to all the cop leadership related to us, to convene a council of war against the Krontzky at Pop's restaurant on West Belmont at 0800…8 am. I need to brief them on the letter, if they have seen any of the Krontzky cronies crawling around and…what we need to do to neutralize the bulk of Alexi's family. After that, I'm letting them go do their thing…while I go over to the Red Square Spa and pick a fight with good ole' Alexi."

"I think you have this all wrapped up; just Krontzky and Ma have no clue. Hey Pam, Pop was pretty shook up before we left. Is there something else you're not telling me?" Funny thing about lawyers, they're an inquisitive bunch. Pam looks to me as if she needs my permission.

I nod to her and let her…inform Thea about her suffering, "Before we came here today, I had two physicals performed by two different OB-GYNs.

"Thea…because of Charlie's abuses at the time, I'm…unable to have my own children." Pam's sad eyes confirm this as Thea's reaction…let's just say the shock and agony of not being able to bear children…Thea's sympathies are felt around the table. She and Pam sob as Thea holds Pam in her embrace. Now I wish I could go back in time and kill Charlie Dupree myself.

"Oh Pam, I'm sorry baby sister. What can I do to help?" Pam knows Thea's asking from the instinct of a big sister looking out for her little sister. "Pam, please tell me you haven't told Ma."

"No, I haven't told Ma. If I did that, she…would…disown me; thinking she was doing me a favor." And given Maria's recent behavior, I don't blame Pam for not telling Maria.

Thea nods, "I agree–the less Ma knows at this point; the better for all of us! What can I do to expedite this operation along?"

Pam shakes her head as I add to the discussion. "I have a suggestion and even our visiting police chief and federal agent will approve; as an attorney, you sometimes do pro bono work for clients who need solid representation right?" Thea nods and I believe she sees where I'm going with this. "Jason and I need you to represent Sgt. Murphy to the Cook County District Attorney's office in filing a harassment suit against Cook County Asst. District Attorney Angelo Constantine for failure to adhere to federal guidelines involving material witnesses. Furthermore, Sgt. Murphy will also be filing a slander suit against the same Asst. District Atty. Constantine for continued verbal abuses sustained on behalf of…one Maria Constantine Papadakis."

Thea gets taken aback by the charges and legal assertions. "Wow, even my mother? If this doesn't get her to calm down, I don't know what will. Someone will have to tell Pop and Uncle Sal about this little legal leap-frogging."

"I'll get your Uncle Rudy to do that." I love how Jason steps in to manage an awkward situation.

Jennifer remained silent through all this discussion. Now, she sounds off.

"I believe we need to hold off on charges where Maria's concerned until we have no other choice. She's demonstrated in the past her…accusations aren't too reliable."

Thea agrees, "That's true, going after Angelo's ambitions sends a clearer message this is not a game you guys playing…but, it's for keeps."

"And maybe when Ma sees my sister's not afraid to go after Angelo for his ambitions, she might take a hint and knock it off for a change." I can tell this part of the operation is making Pam nervous, and she's not alone. "You know, we need to get Thea back home and go get some sleep. We have a long day tomorrow."

Just as we rise to leave, the FSB kids appear again, and the cute and cuddly Agent Brezhnev leads the pack. "Mr. Hampton, we meet again; and I see your group has grown. Where is Sgt. Murphy?"

"If the drama has followed the usual course, he's on his way home to Corpus Christi and will return when the time is right." Jason speaks to Murph's absence and catches the attention of the lovely Russian spy.

"NCIS Special Agent in Charge of Task Force Corpus Christi Jason Vaughn. I didn't expect such a delicious morsel to appear here."

However as Tatyana Brezhnev shimmies up to Jason, Jennifer steps between her and Jason. There are times jealousy and a wolfish attitude will deflect any female desiring to cause trouble. Brezhnev sees the intense, deadly glare in Jennifer's eyes and slowly backs off. "Agent Brezhnev, I am Jennifer Vaughn–Katerina Petrov's eldest sister." Before Brezhnev or any of her people could draw their weapons, Jennifer had her Ladies Smith and Wesson five-shot pistol under Brezhnev's jaw ready to shoot. "Ah, ah; don't get too frisky sugar. Being I'm from the US state of Georgia, I'm one of those Peaches that when someone threatens my family, I get a mighty itchy trigger finger…Ms. Brezhnev.

"Don't get it in your head to try and find them Ms. Brezhnev; that old woman who gave birth to me and Katerina, she's deadlier at this age than she ever was during the Cold War."

"I see; she didn't happen to inform you where she was going?"

Jennifer's chuckle should inform our Russian kewpie doll no one will tell her a damned thing. But Jennifer is honest to a fault. "No, my mother didn't tell me and for that matter, I told her not to tell me where they were going. So you can go back to your boss or bosses and tell them there are no answers I can give you. But know this; you come after the Papadakis, Constantine or any other family related to those families; you will have a severe problem. You will have thirty-seven hundred members of Chicago's Finest reign hell fire down on you and your allies. Make the smart play, Tatyana, go back to Krontzky and tell him what I told you and stop this confrontation. Or we will stop it; with you and yours…in body bags!"

Wow, I expect that kind of death threat from me, Jason, or Pam; not from sweet Police Chief Jennifer Vaughn. Then again, if some Russian crime family put my family through a similar hell, I might experience some kind of negative personality change. And if you could see the sheer terror in the eyes of Tatyana Brezhnev, you would understand she got the message the first time. When the other members of Task Force Corpus Christi stand up, the Russians take this as a sign to leave and not return. Then Pam goes over and hugs the Coltranes, McCoys, Boop Garcia and Quid. "You guys find all the Krontzky business holdings?"

Quid smiles like a rat that stole a block of cheddar cheese. "We all ended up converging on the Red Square Spa. Seems the Krontzky's have little or no imagination at all." She defers to Darius about holdings.

"Just three," Darius Coltrane adds to the discussion. "The Brezhnev's, like Jason and Joe's little girlfriend that just left." There are times Darius' jokes leave little to be desired.

"The other two families involved; one is the Krontzky and the other…Kirov." The last name makes every cop and agent in the room take notice. "Oh yeah, I figured that name would be wired to everyone's hot button."

"And after he escaped, Marko Kirov never surfaced. I hope my parents and Kat got away clean." Jennifer's worry isn't without merit. Knowing how the Kirov is associated with the Krontzky and the Brezhnev will help us decide how we approach everything. "Lightning, I have to ask; Kirov appear anywhere on your radar?"

And when I see Lightning smile like he did when we were in Bosnia, it's going to be a great evening. "Jen, he got into town today. He's been cruising Greek Town all day according to some of the uniforms that frequent that area of business. I told them he impersonated a Marine Corps MP officer and he's wanted in connection to R.I.C.O. violations with the Kirov family of St. Petersburg, Russia. I spoke with Pam's uncle Sal Constantine over at the Intelligence Unit; he said he'll text me if they find him. If they do, they will inform us and he's ours."

"Lightning?" Pam asks him, "Call him and ask him if he's heard from my cousin Ariel or Nikki about a council of war tomorrow morning at Papa Papadakis' Restaurant on West Belmont?" Lightning calls and then hangs up a moment later. "He knows?"

Lightning nods, "He'll be there in the morning."

"Good," Pam looks around and watches Thea intently. Then she says, "Guys, follow us over to my sister's building."

"Pam, you're scaring me!" Thea says quickly.

"Sorry; let's move now!"

We drive over and find nothing out of the ordinary. Pam scans the area around the Arkadia Apartment Building and sees no placards denoting diplomatic vehicles. "Move cautiously. Thea, call Mike and see what's up?"

Thea calls Mike, "Hi babe; have we had any…incursions from the Ottoman Empire of late?"

Every cop family has their own language when a family member might be in a hostage situation. In Jason's family, the captors are called blue-bellies. In my family, we call them Frogs…denoting the French during the Napoleonic Wars. With Greek families, it's always the Turks from the Ottoman Empire.

Thea listens as Mike explains the issue like a video game called *Forge of Empires.* So I gather by her expressions, it's serious. "Okay, I'll let the resistance know; stay safe." She hangs up and tells us. "There are three of them upstairs. They claim they have permission from the local FBI office to question Pam about the whereabouts of one of their citizens. And the part that aggravates me, you already told them you don't know anything."

"Yeah but unless you provide some sort of indisputable proof, Russians believe squat," Jason shakes his head as Pam looks at mapping out a rescue operation. "What do you need from former SEAL Team Three Pammy Pam?"

Thea looks oddly at Pam as Pam smiles at us. "I need a top sniper. Jace, I need you to shoot; babe…you spot for him."

Of course I feign mock insult. "Care to tell me why the Stud and not your favorite Longhorn?"

Pam gives me a reasonable explanation. "I know you love my family like your own. But because we were drawn into this little situation helping them out. I need the *Siddha* to shoot as penance for the risks we took."

"Because if this gets screwed up, I'm to blame for it going south and you're not." Jason smiles as do I. "Come on Devil Dog; let's go kill some Turks!"

Pam and Jennifer shake their heads as Thea looks at them. "Jason and Joe were both snipers in Desert Storm and Bosnia?"

Pam looks at Thea as Jason and I get into position. "You remember when we came here for Thanksgiving; and Joe told the story about an American sniper the Iraqis called the Siddha?" Thea nods as we leave, "The Arabic word Siddha, translates into English Specter.

40

"And when it comes to multiple threats in an enclosed space, Jason's the best sniper we have!"

Six

We get into position where I can use an infrared scope to peek into Thea's apartment. We setup at the top of 820 West Jackson cattycorner to Thea's apartment. The near one hundred yard distance gives Jason his shooting gallery and me a chance to see how he works up close. Darius handed him an M-25 sniper rifle and a full cartridge of 7.62 mm ammo. Jason calmly sets up on the window as I tap into communications for both of us. "Wolf Lair to Wolf Pack, sitrep over?"

"D-Train all clear on Halsted."

"Goddess all clear corner of Jackson and Halsted."

"Irish Lass in position."

"Lightning ready to serenade." We thought a good cover for Leah and Lightning would be to sing an Irish love song to Mike and the boys. Why; only a Greek mom married to an Irish lawyer would want her men to receive an Irish love song as a gift. And a Russian would find it extremely odd.

"Betty Boop monitoring it all."

"Mama Cass clear in the lobby."

"Chi-girl keeping it real."

"She-Wolf to Wolf's Lair, we have bogeys at 10 o'clock. Need backup!" Moments later, Darius and Pam removed two of the three interlopers as Quid put a sleeper hold on the third. *"We're clear Wolf's Lair!"*

"Night Wolf copy," Jason says into his mic as he looks at the bay window on the fourth floor of the apartment. "Standby have movement; Lightning, Lass…go!" When we hear *Irish Eyes* being sung by Lightning, Jason dopes his scope; adjusts his scope so he can hit where he aims. "Give me wind direction and speed please?"

I look through my spotter scope and write down the measurements. Then I relay them to Jason.

"Wind, south by southeast; speed ten nautical. Have a barometer of twenty-two point nine." Jason adjusts again since the barometric pressure and humidity just change.

"Copy," Jason simply says as he sees the front door open.

"Standby people," I say as Lightning begins his serenade with Leah providing harmony. One of the Russians yells to go away. Then Leah's silencer shot goes through the Russian's heart.

Suddenly, we hear Brezhnev yell as Jason sent three shots in rapid succession into the apartment's window. He hits the two remaining males as Lightning and Leah yell, *Wolf Lair, wolf lair…Irish pack leader and cubs safe. Female Turk is in custody!"*

"All units move in, repeat move in!" I shake Jason's hand as he puts the rifle back into its case. "Nice shooting Tex!"

Jason's smile speaks volumes. "Thanks a bunch…Cowboy!" We both laugh as Jason sends out the message. "Night Wolf to Wolf Pack; pack it in we're on our way back."

Moments later, I go up and patch the window Jason shot through and assess any damage he caused. The only expensive piece of furnishing or equipment damaged was Thea's fifty-inch flat-screen TV. "Oh man!" Thea shakes her head as she sees the shattered screen of her TV.

"Hey sis; don't worry…Jason will replace it," Pam smiles as Jason nods.

He walks up to Thea and winces. "Sorry about your TV Thea."

"Small price to pay for keeping my guys safe; thanks Jason."

"Anytime Thea," Jason smiles as Pam walks up and pats him on the back. "Tatyana moved just as the third shot went through the window. I guess she thinks she can plan on avenging their deaths. You and Joe going back to the station?"

"No, I think he and I need to stay here in case more of Krontzky's associates show up. Quid kept her bags in the SUV with ours. She said she'd park on the sofa to make sure we have the front door watched."

I nod to Pam as we see Mike and Thea take in a deep breath of confidence. "Jace, after the council of war in the morning; if you happen to find young Kirov, plant his ass please?"

Jason smiles, "Already working on it Pam. If I may suggest?" Pam nods. "Just as you know little of the Comanche culture; I am just as clueless concerning the Greek culture here. But if I've learned anything from each culture I've experienced; two items of life prevail over all others. Love of family and loyalty to the same. Pam, your mom screwed up royally. She thought by hanging on to that letter from Krontzky, she was protecting you. In retrospect; she almost got thirty-seven hundred cops and their extended families killed. Before you disown her, check, and see what's she's really scared of Pam. There might be a medical reason for her irrational fears."

I see Pam smile as well as nod. I believe my old friend Jason Vaughn said something that might explain Maria's nightmare behavior. And it's a concept neither she nor I thought of in the last eighteen hours. "You're right; at my mother's age, she might suffer from some ailment that would cause this behavior in her. And Krontzky took advantage of a vulnerable old woman. Another reason to find young Kirov and plant his ass!"

A knock at the door comes as every adult with a gun permit draws their side arm. Pam goes up and looks through Thea's peephole. A fleshly hand covers the peephole. Pam motions Thea to ask, "Who is it?"

"Police…open up please?" the muffled voice of Capt. Rudy Papadakis echoes from the hallway as Pam opens the door. Rudy and some of his riot gear-clad officers from the FBI Violent Crimes Task Force roll on inside. "We were told Thea's family was being held hostage." The Rudy sees the shattered screen on the TV and the bullet holes along with the blood on the carpet. "I'm guessing it's been handled?" And Rudy's angry glare does little to scare Pam in her already fatigued state.

"TFCC agents were already here to tuck us in for the night. The threat neutralized, live adversaries arrested and a copy of the paperwork for your records Capt. Papadakis."

Rudy takes the report and puts on his glasses. After he reads it over, Rudy removes his glasses and nods. "Okay, pack it in guys. Someone leave me a sedan so I can get back home please?" All of Rudy's people leave and he stays. "I'm sorry for the disturbance Thea; Maria called the District and told us you were in danger. And she purposely left Pam out of the discussion."

Pam motions *of course she left me out, I'm dead to her!* Thea shakes her head. "Pam's friends at Task Force Corpus Christi arrived in town today. The Vaughn's troubles with the Kirov and Krontzky families prompted them to fly in under the radar. Hence why you didn't know another federal task force was here in Chicago Uncle Rudy."

"Ma may have a condition," Pam adds as Rudy glares at her. "Fine, you think I'm some disloyal, arrogant child. Maybe I am, but I'm not wrong. And if you have the balls to show up at tomorrow's war council Marine!" Pam never disrespects her uncles or her father, but Rudy pushes issues like Maria does sometimes. "I'll prove to you, just how much danger you're in…Captain!" Pam grabs her over shirt and heads out.

I shake my head as Rudy walks up to me. "What the hell is wrong with her Joe? She disowns her mother, practically almost knocks Angelo out of oblivion and now, she' getting help from Vaughn's task force from Texas? Help me understand her please!"

Where do I begin with Rudy asking me that? "The reason the Krontzky family is on your radar currently, and why they are threatening your family; my PI firm assisted Jason and Jennifer with a little family problem…" And I told Rudy the whole story. How Jennifer met Katerina Svetlana Petrov, how Col. Kirov and the Krontzky family were involved and now why Maria's actions threaten thirty-seven hundred cops related to him.

"…originally, we flew up here to check on the situation involving Sgt. Murphy. Now we believe one of these Russian families killed Chief Murphy and his family; then setup the scenario to pin it on Frank."

"And Maria held a threatening letter from Pam so she couldn't accurately gauge the threat? Oh my God; why wouldn't Maria give it to Sal or me?" Rudy shakes his head and now realizes Pam's actions and a call to arms for the family; he understands why Pam excluded everyone up to this point. "I think Pam's right; something's wrong with Maria. Tell Pam I'll be there on West Belmont at 0800 sharp."

"Thank you…Uncle Rudy," Pam returns, smiles weakly as she leans up against the hallway corner. "Other than Joe, his family and the cop family I have in Texas; this is all I have left Rudy. I'm not able to do any more than that."

Rudy's expression personifies confusion. Pam and Thea look at each other and Pam nods as she goes back down the hallway. Thea turns to Rudy, "She went to two gynecologists prior to this trip. Uncle Rudy, Pam can't have children."

"Meaning…she's physically unable to have children…safely?" I nod as Rudy holds back from slamming his hand against a wall. "Her ex, Charlie, where is he?"

"Dead; Pam and I had been already dating when he arrived in Dallas during a missing person's case. He broke in and she shot him dead. The Dupree are memory; like the Russians will be soon Rudy." I define the solution adequately.

"Good," Rudy says as he looks off into the night. "One less worry for me or the family."

"However, Uncle Rudy; until we get the Russians under wraps, you still have the extra worry." Of course I might be overstating it a bit, but it keeps everyone focused on the task and less on Greek family drama.

Almost midnight and I finally walk into Thea's guestroom where Pam and I stay.

I crawl into bed after I wash part of the long day off. When I roll over to kiss Pam good night, she's smiling at me. "Hey beautiful, I thought you might have nodded off already.

"You don't get that lucky Longhorn," Pam smiles as she kisses me. When she slides her fit body over mine, I realize I'm overdressed. "Um…what's with the underwear…my handsome Longhorn?"

"I walked in and my fatigue overrode my honeymooner's judgment. My apologies Mrs. Hampton," I smile as she slides my shorts off. Then something stiff arose; and it might be me. "You…approve of the rise to the occasion?"

"I love it when…pillars of desire make themselves known to a newlywed wife." I love it when my little Greek goddess of law enforcement talks dirty to me.

0600 rolls around as we get up and get dressed. Denim is the order of the day for both of us and matching pairs of black Justin Roper cowboy boots. When we head into the kitchen, Thea and Mike are up and Thea hands us each a cup of Greek coffee. "Denim all the way; now that's true love." Thea's remark makes us laugh. And as I look over at Mike, he reminds me of blue-eyed Irish Army JAG lawyer I knew in Bosnia. "Joe, what's wrong?"

"Oh…nothing; I keep thinking ever since I met Mike, I'd seen him somewhere before. Were you ever a member of the Army's Judge Advocate General Corps?"

Mike answers me, "I was a JAG lawyer with 101st Airborne Division from Fort Campbell, Kentucky. I did three tours in Bosnia and between my first and second, I married Thea."

"And I will tell you now Pam; Ma had a shit-fit when she found out I was marrying an Irishman. A lot of the men from Greek Town she wanted to marry me off to; were some of the greasiest slobs I'd ever seen. I told her, '*You may disown me if you wish, but I'm not marrying any of those clowns.*'"

"Then you marry Mike and it all went downhill from there huh?" Pam asks as Thea laughs. Moments later, both of the boys each a mini-me of Mike, walk in. "Hey fellas, what got you two out of bed?"

Liam the oldest, walks up and hugs Pam, "We didn't want you to go without wishing you well Aunt Pam."

"Yeah Aunt Pam; we don't get to see you that often," Sean says as he hugs Pam after she bends down. "Aunt Pam, does Uncle Joe hug kids?"

Pam's mouth falls wide open as does Thea's. Apparently, I haven't performed my duties as the affectionate uncle. So while Pam and Thea have the boys distracted, I sneak up behind them and give them a big, Texas bear hug...both of them! Short and skinny Irish boys are better hugged in groups so they can feel the family love. "Okay, are you guys convinced I like hugging you two?"

"Yeah, we guess so," Liam answers for his brother as I playfully headlock both of them. And I'm doing all of this on one sip of coffee; that's weird even for me! Must be that strong Greek coffee.

Pam walks up and rubs both their scalps with her knuckles. "Ow, Aunt Pam!"

"Well you guys question whether or not Uncle Joe and I love you guys. Would we, Uncle Joe and I; show up here with Aunt Laquita and federal task force, just so some Russian bad guys, don't make Baklava out of you two...if we didn't love you two?"

You could see the shame in their eyes as they lower their heads. I give Pam a low stare as Thea and Mike snicker quietly. I let them off the hook. "Hey guys, I know you guys love us a bunch. So, we love you two just as much. And maybe one day, we get your folks to take some time off their busy caseloads and have you guys joined us in Texas. We can go horseback riding, rope and punch some doges; we might even do some deep sea fishing in the Gulf of Mexico!"

"Aunt Pam told us your uncle; "Big Jake" Stockton owned a family ranch outside Dallas. Is that true?"

"Yes, it is Sean. I spent my youth on that ranch; riding horses and helping my grandpa raise horses and cattle. And after Aunt Pam and I came home from our honeymoon, Uncle Jake wanted to know when you two cowpokes were going to visit?"

Thea dropped down to one knee and hugged her boys, "You know, if you two will help me pack your suitcases, we'll go to Texas today and visit Uncle Jake. Would you guys like that?"

"Yeah!" the boys cry out as all three run to the back of the apartment and begin packing.

I see Mike standing over by the counter smiling and shaking his head. "One thing I know I can count on in this world is that I love Thea and my sons. But last night, you showed me I can count on you to be a great brother-in-law, and show my kids there is life outside of Greek Town; even outside of Chicago. Pam realized long ago; she had to get out in order to love where she came from. Pam loves her family, and she taught me a great deal about loving Thea the right way. And as a result, along comes Liam and Sean." Then Mike looks at both of us. "Pam, Joe; find these bastards that tried to take my family from me last night!"

Pam hugs Mike and whispers, "We're working on it Mike. Enjoy your vacation." When Thea and the kids came out with the luggage, Quid smiles and grabs the luggage for the boys. "Quid, the boys got this!"

"No, no, no, and no; if my little buddies are headed to Texas, someone needs to assist them in getting to the airport." Quid has a point; we want to get Mike, Thea, and the boys to Texas as quickly as possible. And this helps her with family issue situations from a protective standpoint. "Am I taking them to Midway International?"

"Yes," I say as Pam nods. "Boop's waiting at the Signature Flight Terminal to help you get them aboard. Quid, we need you to escort them to Love Field and come back. I have a funny feeling."

"Will your uncle or brother meet us at Love Field?" Quid asks pointedly.

"John will meet you as well as an old Marine Corps staff named Wade McKenzie. Tell him you're the XO with the Provost Office at NAS Corpus Christi. If he asks, tell him Capt. Joe Hampton sends his regards."

"How well do you and your brother know this guy, McKenzie?" Quid asks mysteriously.

"Wade helped us out on the missing ranch foreman case Pam, and I worked together. Wade and some of the homeless Marines in the downtown Dallas area helped us track someone related to the case. We hired a bunch of those guys and gals so they could feel more…back home." I put the situation into perspective as Quid nods. "Why do you ask?"

"He was one of the DI's at Command School. I thought McKenzie was pretty cool cat. Nice to know he finally came home right."

Seven

We arrive at Papa Papadakis' Restaurant on West Belmont at 0745. By now, Thea and her family are on their way to Love Field in Dallas to go spend time at the Stockton Ranch. To my surprise, I catch Uncle Jake having his morning coffee. "Well, what do you know you old ornery cuss?"

"Oh you know me; trying to keep all these jokers on the ranch in line!" I know that's a fact as Uncle Jake and I laugh about his joke. *"What prompts you to call me so early in the morning?"*

"Did Pam mention to Cody yesterday some of her family wanted to visit the ranch?"

"Yes; something about some issue that followed you guys from March. Which of her relatives ended up someone's target?"

"Her sister Athena, her husband Mike Flynn and their boys Liam and Sean. John and Wade agreed to pick them up at Love Field and take them to Denton."

"Cody got a call from John; they will land in an hour. Don't worry Joe; we'll look after them here. You and Pam get those issues resolved there."

"Thanks Uncle Jake," then I said something I never thought I'd say to him. "Love you Uncle!"

I could hear the tears in Uncle Jake's voice. *"Love you too kid; watch your ass!"*

"Always!" I hang up as Pam walks out with mild shock in her eyes. "Yes ma'am?"

"You just tell Jake you loved him?" I nod. "Oh lord, it's getting weird!"

"You think that's weird; look at the fact I learned my father was MI-6 before his years as Chief Constable...that's weird!"

0800, Pam and I finish our coffee and our pastries from our breakfast as she calls the council of cops to order. "Welcome all officers named Papadakis, Constantine, Aniston, Flynn, and Kapelos. Our five families represent one-third of the total strength of CPD and surrounding county sheriff's departments. I called this family…war council to present to all of us a threat to our very families."

Adam Kapelos, Undersheriff of Cook County asks, "What threat, Cousin Pam?" Adam's Mediterranean good looks distinguish his Asia Minor heritage. "How wide-spread is this threat?"

"We have three Russian Mob families trying to obtain information on a young Russian woman, who immigrated to the US in March. One of these families promised her as a product of their human trafficking interests to the chief family…the Krontzky. The reason: a feud between the Kirov and another Russian family named Petrov. Our family is threatened, because Joe and I protected the young woman while her family worked out another deal with the Krontzky. The Krontzky reneged."

"So you are to blame for this trouble!" Argyle Flynn, Mike's father yelled in response as the crowd erupted in debate. And it seems like the families wasted a good half hour before I spoke with Gus.

Then I fired my Sig and shot a hole in the ceiling. Sometimes, firing a loaded weapon is more effective than the traditional dairy whistle approach. I yell, "That's enough!" I keep my Sig in my hand to accent I'm not playing around. I know it takes a lot to get my family's attention at times, but Pam warned me once I might have to do this. "It doesn't matter who is to blame for these Russians threatening the family; the question is do you want to stop blaming whoever and do something about it?"

"What about this Sgt. Murphy issue?" Uncle Sal will not let this go. So Pam marches down from the dais and gets right in his face.

"NCIS is handling that one! If you mention it again, Sgt. Constantine, you will be suspended for sixty days without pay!

"And that comes from your Chief of Detectives!" Wow, watching Pam work a room like a Marine Corps DI does have its attention-getting moments. Just then, Chief Superintendent Patrick Brown walks in. "Room tench-hut!" Every cop stands at attention as Superintendent Brown walks up to a saluting Pam. "Good morning Superintendent!"

"Good morning Captain Hampton; welcome back home!"

"Thank you, sir!"

"I see you've assembled your task force Captain; but I also heard the dissention as well. Maybe what needs to happen, is at the behest of the mayor, I temporarily name you as an Asst. Chief Super for this department!" Murmurs around the room continue as even Uncle Sal sits in stunned silence. "Yes, Sgt. Constantine; your niece Captain Hampton, has that power and authority. All she has to do is call the Chief of D's and you're benched! NCIS is handling the Chief Murphy investigation; drop it! Do you understand me Sgt. Constantine?"

"Yes sir." The defeat in Sal's voice is deafening but deserved. He's been told a bunch of times in the last twenty-four hours to drop the Murphy case. Now that Pam has a temporary promotion for CPD; maybe the difficult family members in the room will take her seriously. "If I may sir, my sister's...concerned due to my niece's safety. That's why she keeps insisting Murphy's part of the problem."

"And I can sympathize Sergeant; but if a federal agency such as NCIS invokes their authority into a case like that one, CPD must comply with that order or by subject to appropriate penalties; do you understand Sal?" Chief Superintendent Brown looks sadly into Sal's eyes as Sal nods. "What is this all about...really?"

"Maria's...suffering from Dementia." Pam's mouth falls wide open and extends her hands out to her sides. "We'll talk more about it later...Acting Asst. Chief Super Hampton."

"Damned right we will...Sgt. Constantine."

Pam quietly makes her way back up to the dais. "Now that we've established the chain of command; you all took a number between one and five when you entered. After you meet with the family member designated with the large plaques of numbers, you will return to your respective districts and prepare to execute the operation. You will get details from your task force supervisors indicated by the numbers. Are there any questions?" Angelo attends the meeting; possibly hoping to be a nuisance somehow. That didn't surprise me. "Yes Mr. Constantine?"

"How do the local county attorney's offices coordinate with the U.S. Attorney's office in Chicago?"

"That's a good question Mr. Constantine; the A-USA is speaking with the House and Senate Judiciary Committees in Washington as we speak. The concern we're facing is these three crime families have direct ties to the Russian Federal Security Bureau; meaning we may be able to use FISA (US Foreign Intelligence Surveillance Act) warrants, putting this matter to bed once and for all. We are receiving reports from NCIS, FBI and to include the CIA as well as NSA. I would wait for info from the lead A-USA before acting on anything. But share information so we can speed up this process."

"So, for example, local District Attorney's investigators see these guys doing something…illegal, we should defer to the A-USA? What if shots are fired?"

"Are you anticipating doing something to provoke shots being fired…Angelo?" Pam's irritation makes Angelo smile; he's fishing for an angle.

Time for me to add to the discussion. "Mr. Constantine; based on my years of experience as a former federal agent, failure to exercise extreme good judgment when an A-USA has defined what we call, terms of engagement, you will be arrested and subject to charges up to and including…disbarment! You…desire to…push your luck; do so to your own detriment."

"Does that help to answer your question…Angelo?" Pam stands and places her hands on the podium.

"And I strongly suggest you nod 'yes' and not say another word. Or Captain Papadakis will walk over and arrest you for obstruction of a multi-level federal investigation...clear?" Angelo nods quickly and exits as fast as Sal looks up at Pam and chuckles. "Check in with your task force supervisors prior to leaving and...good hunting!" As the breakfast meeting with family task force breaks up, Pam goes back over to Uncles Sal and Rudy. "Why does he act like some knot-headed goo bah?"

Sal just shakes his head. "He's ambitious; I never said he was smart about exercising his ambitions. And given the fact you punched his lights out yesterday after he tried to refile that Murder One charge on Murphy; he feels justified in irritating you. He knows I won't touch him unless he does something illegal, but he also knows pushing you will cost him everything if he continues."

"And as much as I hate to say this Sal, I hope Angelo does screw up!" Rudy's comment makes Sal turn and glare at him. "Did the two of you know about the threatening letter Maria received in April from the Krontzky family?" Before Sal answers, Rudy clarifies how serious it is, "And I'll know if you're lying to me or not; I've known you that long Sal."

Sal throws up his hands. "Okay, I knew Murphy was coming to Chicago because I learned of his family's murder the day before yesterday. The Krontzky sent me a letter as well; telling me to frame Murphy to keep Maria and her family safe. If not, everyone got plugged...you too Pam."

Pam shakes her head as she calls on her earwig. "Jason, come in here with Darius and Lightning please?" Jason appears with Darius Coltrane and Lightning McCoy. "Uncle Sal and my cousin Angelo are now material witnesses in this investigation. Have TFCC agents detain Angelo until he can be questioned by me!"

Sal yells, "Why can't you just be loyal to your family for once? For once, stop being a by-the-book cop?"

Pam turns back to Sal before she leaves and delivers the *rip* of her life.

"Detective Salvatore Constantine; I am giving you a fifteen day rip for your last comment. In addition, you are indefinitely suspended without pay until the conclusion of this case. You hand me your star and side arm now." Pam holds out her hand as Sal does as she commands. "Captain Papadakis, you will lift the suspension of Det. Ariel Papadakis and inform her she will function as the acting command sergeant of the Intelligence Unit. Take Uncle Sal home and inform Aunt Sophie; he's not working because he made a stupid decision! Get him out of here!"

"Let's go Sal," Rudy said quietly as Gus walks over. "Despite the fact Sal is angry like Maria; Pam's doing the job right Gus. Don't fault her for sticking to her guns on this matter."

"I'm not; to love this large family she has by taking on the responsibility she's been handed and not by choice, Pamela's doing what God meant her to do." And then Gus looks intently into Sal's eyes. "You and my wife call my daughter the cop...disloyal; and pull a bullshit stunt like this one, both of you? What the hell were you thinking Salvatore?"

"I was trying to protect this family; no matter the cost!" Sal just shakes his head as he looks into Rudy's and Gus's eyes. "Maria...married into the right family. My son and I are too much like my old man; we're opportunists and could care less who it hurts in the long run. And maybe I'm angry at Pamela because she's right; and she does this job right. And I wish I were more like her...the best cop of us."

Then I watch as Chief Superintendent Brown walks up to the in-laws who serve as cops. "You know Sal, if you go over there and tell her that; I could be persuaded to get her to reconsider part of the discipline she just meted out to you a moment ago. Look at it this from her point of view Sal; she works for a female boss who herself, is persecuted by people because: she's been drugged in college against her will. And that's just the starting line for Jennifer Vaughn..."

Brown goes on to tell all the horrors Jennifer suffered as a cop over the last twenty years of her career. When I look again, Sal's in tears because he realizes the loyalty and family feeling Jennifer Vaughn inspires in Pam. "You see; there's a difference in how loyalty is demanded or asked. You demanded it because of your age and position in your family; but…she never gives it…why?"

Sal smiles. "Because how we do the job has changed…and I'm one of those old farts that stayed the same. And I demanded…what I didn't deserve."

"And when Pam receives loyalty; it's not because she demands it. Pam receives loyalty because of how she does the job and inspires those around her to do the job right. And that Sal, that is true loyalty as well as integrity. Look at it another way: if you can't be twice the cop she is, given your years of experience, you shouldn't expect her to be half the cop you are when you make unreasonable demands. Food for thought." Then Chief Superintendent Brown goes over and hugs my short wife and disappears amongst the breakfast crowd.

Then as if Hera, Queen of Olympus sashays past a hall of heroes, Pam walks over to Rudy and Sal. "Give us a moment please Captain?" Rudy sees me appear next to her, looks to Sal, smiles, and then gives us space. Then I kiss Pam on the cheek and give them space as well. "Sgt. Constantine?"

"Acting Asst. Chief Super Hampton; I would like to…apologize for my less than professional behavior earlier. I was wrong to call you disloyal when I had no concept of what loyalty actually means." Pam stands by, more patient than I would be had it been my uncle calling me disloyal…and has. "And under the circumstances, I deserved every ounce of rebuke and discipline you meted out moments ago. And I can only explain my actions and attitude this way; I'm an old cop who's set in his ways and forgot time moved on; and there's no excuse for that."

"I agree," Pam looks into Sal's eyes. "But I sense you have more to say to me sir."

58

"You're correct; I do," I see Sal straining to get the words out, but it's a long time not being said, and now is as good time as any to say them. "When you told me that you planned to keep Angelo and me as material witnesses, I only saw my little Pamela, acting like some spoiled child getting her way. What I should have seen, is a police captain who has inspired officers under her command to do this job right. And the inspiration to do the job right, despite the consequences, is true loyalty; on the job and in a family."

"You're right; you don't deserve an ounce of a break due to all the crap I just dumped on top of your pointed noggin. However, in light of the most well-spoken and well-crafted apology you've probably ever made in your life to anyone, you're probably needed worse at your district than being in custody as a material witness. Here, your star and side arm…Sgt. Constantine."

Sal smiles as he looks at his sergeant's star. "Thank you and…keep Angelo wherever you plan to keep him."

"So I don't shoot him myself?" Pam asks with an impish grin.

"Yes, that too!" Sal laughs with her.

Eight

We return to NS Great Lakes as Darius and Jason begin questioning or attempting to question Tatyana Brezhnev. Inside the observation room, with the rest of TFCC, sits Jennifer, Leo Vale, and someone no one expected Pam's Cousin Angelo. Jason sits in front of Brezhnev as Darius stands under the video camera. *"Agent Brezhnev, you were ordered by your superiors as well as Col. Kirov's men to leave the United States three months ago. Why have you not complied with those orders?"*

Her answer almost makes me ill. *"We were under the impression, due to Sgt. Murphy's discussions prior to his arrival in Chicago, Katerina Svetlana Petrov was here. It seems; we were in error."*

"In error enough to murder Master Chief Petty Officer Daniel Murphy and MCPO Murphy's family; is that your story Madam Brezhnev?" Darius asks as he leans in over the petite Russian blonde. *"No one in the families you targeted in the last three months knows of Miss Petrov's location. No one on our task force, no one in the Vaughn family, no one related to the Hamptons of Texas; not even the Marines you've tried to falsely accuse of treason to our country. Chief Vaughn's parents have vanished with Miss Petrov. You have drawn attention where you shouldn't."*

"Perhaps this Murphy had, how do you say it, an…accomplice to this crime?" Brezhnev smiles as she tries to read Jason's blank expression. *"You think I'm pretty…Comrade Vaughn?"*

"No, not one bit. You're as ugly as sin. Wait, you asked me about your looks. Well, of course you're pretty. However, I prefer the beauty of one's spirit these days. So that seduction ploy you just tried to use; I'm immune. Plus, I have video surveillance footage of your team first inside MCPO Murphy's apartment twenty-four hours prior to CCPD Det. Sgt. Murphy's arrival.

"And three hours prior to Murphy arriving in Chicago, we have your team leaving the Murphy apartment. I'm going to run ballistics on your weapons and I'm confident I'll find matches to the slugs we dug out of the walls and ceiling. Plus we found MCPO Murphy's blood on your black gloves Tatyana." Jason has her cold. *"Well?"*

"Lawyer; and I want Athena Flynn to represent me!" Tatyana Brezhnev smiles as if she has us over a barrel. Then Pam walks in and whispers in Jason's ear. After she rises, Pam glares down into Brezhnev's eyes. *"What?"*

Pam's response shocks us all. *"My sister and her family, died in a mid-sir collision somewhere over Missouri. She will not be able to represent you. The FAA discovered a RCIED* (Radio Controlled Improvised Explosive Device) *circuit board tied to a cell phone owned by Marko Kirov. Tell us where he is, and I'll speak to the US Assistant District Attorney about a deal for you."*

"Lawyer, please?" She says with same cold, vicious smile she smiled when we caught her at Thea's apartment.

"They all do the same thing; don't they Agent Vaughn? Just when you get to the good questions, they lawyer up to stay out of jail. Okay, get her a lawyer. Then if it is determined she will not cooperate with us further; charge her with commission of a terrorist act on US soil. The Russian government hates our Patriot Act!"

"Oh yes; lovely little law when dealing with holding people hostage; killing innocent families who have no knowledge of what you seek. And here's the juicy parts Tatyana: no lawyers, or judges. Just put you in a safety orange jumpsuit and ship you off to Cuba; the American side of the island. We can hold you there indefinitely...until you either cooperate or your government raises enough hell with our state department to listen to our grievances concerning your outlaw colleagues. Either way, I don't care. My heart, because you chose to bring this trouble to our doorstep, is colder than the most frigid parts of Russia." Pam smiles her evil grin and nods.

Jason, Darius, and Pam exit the interrogation room and Jason says, "Call an attorney; let's see if they can get her to wise up."

"I doubt it; that's one tough Russian cookie in there," Angelo gazes into the interrogation room and shakes his head. "Did you notice her neck? She has prison tattoos from some lady's gulag. And from what I can tell, she's been through someone's human trafficking pipeline as a victim. She didn't start out as a Russian gangster."

"I know," Pam looks at Angelo's stunned expression. "She was sent through their pipeline as training for her job with the FSB. My option for a Patriot Act case; is the only way I can get her to cooperate and possibly avoid rivers of blood shed from Greek Town, to the Ukrainian Village, to all other points out across Chicago. Do you understand I'm gearing up for a war I can win; but I'd like to avoid that option if at all possible?" Angelo nods. "Good; because I think based on your record, you're an outstanding trial lawyer with the Cook County Attorney's office. But Angelo, some of your personal behavior borders on pedophilia. If you don't grow up, you'll compromise every case you're on in the future."

"Always comes back to that with me; my bad behavior. Seems as I recall, you weren't an angel growing up either…Acting Asst. Chief Super Hampton."

"No I wasn't, but I also learned the hard way in the Corps too Angelo. One mistake; one…childish screw-up, can break a career if you get caught up in it like I was. It's time to stop being a frat boy in college and grow up…Cousin Angelo!"

Then Jason and Jennifer flank Angelo. "And that mime you groped at Pam's wedding in Texas?" Jason asks menacingly, "That's our sixteen-year old daughter!"

Pam almost comes unglued on Angelo. "You groped the mime? Did you lose all your faculties the day of my wedding?"

"I didn't know it was a kid!"

"That's why you never, ever grope women at a wedding jackass!"

Pam's frustration aside, the look in Jason's as well as Jennifer's eyes; well, I fear for Angelo's life expectancy. So Pam puts the ball squarely in the Vaughn's court. "If they decide to press charges, or Gracie's filed a complaint; I can't help you Angelo."

"Oh no worries there Pam," Jennifer's feral smile surfaces. "Gracie simply asked us if we ever found the putz that did that, we were to either scalp or castrate him!" Jennifer's two-inch lock blade pops out. She waves it in front of Angelo. "So, Mr. Putz…choose; hair or balls?"

"Don't you think that's…a little extreme for one mistake?" Angelo smiles nervously as Jennifer slowly and sadistically, waves the knife in front of Angelo and continues her feral smile. "Pam, Pam please talk to her!"

"Oh I might be able to talk her…out of harming you, but if I do…it'll cost ya Cuz!" Pam looks as Jennifer turns to her and winks.

"Anything, I'll do anything please…don't harm the hair or the crown jewels!" Angelo's now crying as Jennifer gives Pam a *whatcha gonna do now* look. Pam carefully considers Angelo's dilemma and she can see Jason trying not to bust out laughing. "If she agrees to not…mutilate you in any manner; you will take a voluntary six month leave of absence from the District Attorney's office and voluntarily enter rehab for sexual addiction. As penance for your excessive groping, you will write letters of apology to every family member, and guest at my wedding you groped. You will also…take three of those six months on leave to work for legal aid helping the underprivileged. Got me?"

"I'll call my boss first thing in the morning," Angelo looks to Pam, who looks to Jennifer, who sighs and puts her knife away. "Thank God!" Jason twists Angelo's right earlobe. "Ouch, ow, ow, ow!" That's a clear, clear sign Jason won't let Angelo off that easy.

"Don't start thanking God just yet Angelo; if I find you in Texas ever again Angelo, I will gather every woman you groped at that wedding.

"Then I will lock you in a room alone with all those women, and if there is anything left of you, then we'll file sexual harassment charges. And your career, as you know it, will be over! You understand me…son?" Angelo nods and runs out as fast as his short legs could carry him. "Actually, that was my contribution in saving his miserable life Pam."

"You mean it wasn't Gracie Angelo groped?" Pam asks as her astonishment permeates the room.

"Nope, someone far more dangerous. You see, Gracie wasn't miming that day; that particular mime was Texas Ranger Valerie Stanton." Jennifer's smile has more devilish purpose than Pam understands. "You didn't get the chance to meet Valerie or her family; but Angelo groped her. And when she found out from your mother, he served as a Cook County Asst. District Attorney; she almost came looking for him to use him as target practice with her Winchester Repeater."

Pam shakes her head, "Was she serious about using Angelo for target practice?"

"When it comes to crime; Valerie's more serious about catching crooks than you!" Jason accents that point by puckering his lips.

Pam puckers her lips and then smiles. "I have to meet this Texas Ranger girlfriend of yours Jen. She sounds like my kind of buddy!"

"She worked another angle for us with Kat's case. The situation never presented itself for you to meet her then or at your wedding; I'm sorry."

"Oh Jen," Pam throws her arms around Jennifer and just hugs her warmly. "I had over three hundred relatives in Corpus that weekend. Ten percent of the total family here. I sent apology letters to the guest I didn't get to meet or speak with at the reception. I felt so out of it after the ceremony and then the reception."

"I thought it was the bachelorette party the night before!" I turn my head toward them. "Uh-oh, I spoke out of turn."

"No you didn't; I always suspected Pam of having a wild night before getting married to me," I smile like a cobra.

"Because Jason treated me to one too!"

"Just how wild was your bachelor party Longhorn?"

I squint at Jason as I grit my teeth. "We played poker dear. And the ladies who attended, tended bar and served us drinks; all manner of drinks."

"Really," Pam accusingly looks to me; then she looks at Jason. "And what other services did these ladies perform while working this…tame party of yours?"

"They allowed us to make use of their costume pieces as poker chips?"

"What?" Pam yells as everyone, me as well, dives for cover. "You mean to tell me this little poker party, was another form of strip poker?"

Now we, my lovely spouse and I, are about to have our first marital spat; and she's spoiling for it. "So let me get this straight; you have an issue concerning our version of strip poker, but you attend an all-male dancer review where they swing their members around for all to see?"

Pam starts to say something; then her eyes widen with shock and she gulps. I give her the evil eye accusation as Jason shakes his head. "And my dear Joseph, let us not forget the honorable Head Hostess, Chief Jennifer Vaughn."

Jennifer sips her coffee in silence as we all playfully glare at her. "What?" She picks up a chocolate-glazed donut and takes a bite. "Seriously what?"

"Come on Jen help me out here…I didn't touch one skin flute the whole night!"

Jennifer looks to Boop, Cass, and Leah about Pam's bachelorette party. "We were all…too drunk to remember." Boop and the rest bury their heads as they head out of the observation room.

"We were all, a little drunk that night. I will not say whether I did anything outside the bounds of my marriage or not; because I don't remember.

"However, I do remember cameras, filming everything. So, in a year or two, we might end up on some porn site!" Jennifer smiles as Jason gives her a less than pleased look. Her smile disappears as Pam walks up behind her. "How dead am I?"

"Oh Chief Vaughn, our husbands won't kill us or do us any harm. Why you ask; because we have thirty-seven hundred cops watching our backs!" Pam smiles and Jennifer joins her.

Then Jason deflates their sails, "That works, until you return to Corpus Christi…ladies." Jason leaves Observation.

And I add, "Dig yourself out of this one smartass!" I smile like an imp as I leave the observation area. I meet up with Jason outside, "You're not really angry about that bachelorette party, are you?"

"No, I'm not Joe; but over twenty years, I've loved and supported Jennifer in everything she did. If I didn't, we found a way to deal with it. And…both, she and I had our wild parties prior to marriage."

I can hear what Jason's saying; he and Jennifer are past that point in their marriage. However, they do find ways to keep it spicy. "Maybe if I return the glare at her once in a while; especially when she over does it like at Pam's bachelorette party, it reminds her she's subjected to the same general temptations I am. I'm not going to fault her for having a little fun and you shouldn't begrudge Pam any fun either brother."

"Pam's a Marine; and I know I say that a bunch, but she is more than that. And I knew that about her back in 2013. Maybe, I have this newlywed husband jealousy working here, but I love her so much." Jason nods and I didn't have to say more; he completely understands my viewpoint. "I just wish I could be the kind of husband she deserves, you know?"

"What are you talking about Joe? Are you a rude, condescending, obnoxious, abusive jerk?" Jason's use of adjectives can blow the mind at times. "Well, are you?"

"Not in a million years; even when I worked with you at NCIS man!" We both laugh as I realize I start to question whether I fit in Pam's life or not.

"You know though, ever since Pam and I hooked up with you and Jen in January, and helped Quid, we saw a bright future. Now, after you and Jen helped me and Pam; we help you guys and then immediately returning the favor again. I guess the four of us…have formed a family of sorts."

"We did, and you as well as Pam will have one of your own." Jason says gently. He knows that Pam's medical issues have a sensitive slant on her personality. "You guys have talked adoption, right?"

"Yeah, but we might adopt kids who are older than five. Kids who are already in school need good homes and families too."

"Your own Hampton's Heroes Platoon Joe?" Jason asks with humor in his voice.

"Yes," it's all I could say is 'yes'. Maybe Pam and I can have a big family with kids from all over and we can teach them how to live together under one roof. Of course, it is an ambitious, but reality might be a brother and sister who need us worse than anyone else. I could see Pam being a mother to two kids like that.

Nine

Pam and Jennifer finally exit the observation area as Jason and I just admire these women we love. Pam and Jennifer look at one another; then us and Jennifer asks, "What's wrong with you two?"

Jason shrugs off the question. "Just thinking about stuff; marriage, family, careers and jobs. How somehow, this little foursome has formed a unique family all its own. And I guess the thing that bugs me; we almost got into a four-way verbal brawl a few minutes ago over a bachelor and bachelorette party…each. We're all human here. Why are we here?"

Pam starts to say, but Jennifer puts her hand on Pam's shoulders. "We came here to back up someone who backed us up three months ago; after we stood up for them a month earlier when they married. And now we share the same Russian problem because my dear, sweet mother; couldn't trust us to make this right. And I am sorry you and Joe were caught up in this Pam."

Pam shrugs the same way Jason did earlier. "It is what it is Jen; however, the Russian's venue to start a rumble…they would have been smarter to do this in Corpus. You see, although I no longer live here, Chi-town is still my town! And I want to evict Brezhnev, Kirov and Krontzky from my town! You guys with me?"

"All the way," Jason and Jennifer smile as they sound off in stereo.

I walk up and kiss my newlywed wife, "I was all in the moment I met you; much less married you Acting Asst. Chief Superintendent Hampton. And now, with two of the best snipers of Desert Storm and Bosnia, we can help serve that eviction notice."

Pam's eyes well up with tears. "Thank you, seems so inadequate but thank you all the same." Then Pam receives a call. "Hampton, say again?" She puts the call on speaker phone. "Okay, go Rudy."

"We discovered ICE had an investigation into the human trafficking end after our meeting broke up. So I reached out; we have some major league fed help. I informed them of your connection with TFCC out of Texas. Agent Longbow told me to tell Jason…Yatahey?"

"Rudy, tell Longbow…híŋhaŋni for me. Basically, I'm telling him 'good morning' in Southern Lakota. He told me basically…the same." Jason's connection with Native American service members always impressed the Brass as he bridged gaps no one dared to bridge at the time. "Rudy, what else is going on?"

"Longbow wanted me to ask if Joe and Pam could take in a couple of American kids who were sold to them by their grandparents in Arkansas. Their father was Greek, believe it or not. Their names are Andromeda and Leonidas Drivas."

"Rudy, did they speak with Cook County Child Services about this case?"

"They did, but Longbow informed them since these kids had no relatives to speak of that wanted them, he informed Child Services these two were material witnesses in our case…lucky us!"

I nod as Pam asks, "Give me your twenty and we'll be over in a jiffy."

An hour later we arrive at a strip mall on North Clark Street less than two blocks from Rudy's District House. We see members of the Brezhnev, Kirov and Krontzky soldiers in charge of human trafficking, walking into a paddy wagon. A dozen other children find relatives in Chicago willing to take them and send them back to their families. There, I spy Rudy and a long-haired Lakota ICE agent Joseph Longbow Hawkins smiling at us. When we were in Bosnia, I was called Big Joe, after my late grandfather and Longbow was called Little Joe. He shakes his head as he sees me and Jason standing next to one another.

"Jason 'Night Wolf' Vaughn; why did you bring that sawed off, crazy-assed Marine with you?"

Jason shakes his head as we all laugh at 'Little' Joe's observations. "Big Joe Hampton; good to see you brother!"

"How ya been man? I never would've imagined you to be an ICE agent. Why ICE?"

Jason laughs after Longbow gives his response, "Well, it's quite a nefarious scheme really." Oh lord, he sounds like a bad actor in a Shakespeare scene. "My plan was to become an ICE agent with the hopes of booting all you European-descended people out of my country!"

"How are you coming along on your scheme to rid us of European descent from these shores?"

"Shh!" Longbow shushes us. "Not so loud dude, I said this was *my* nefarious scheme. Never said it would work!" Everyone laughs as we walk over to the CPD squad car where Andromeda and Leonidas Drivas wait for us. We see the kids; nicknames Romy and Leo. Romy is twelve and Leo ten. Both wore dirty t-shirts, jeans, and tennis shoes with holes in them.

Pam takes one look at their faces and her tears start to fall. Longbow introduces us. "Romy, Leo; these are my friends Joe and Pam. Pam's last name before she married Joe, was Papadakis, same as Rudy's over there."

"Really?" the voice of little Leo sounds mousey but might be due to his treatment. Pam bends down on one knee and looks up into Leo's eyes. "Why are you crying Pam?"

Pam's eyes continue to shed tears as I hunch up next to her. "Leo, right?" I ask and he nods. "Pam…is so…heartbroken because she sees how you've been treated; it makes her cry. And if I'm reading her eyes right, your treatment has really upset her. So, she's having trouble answering you vocally, okay Leo?"

Then Romy reaches out and touches Pam's hand. "We're sorry we don't have clean clothes…Pam, right?"

"That's right Romy," I look into Pam's eyes and she nods. "Captain Papadakis is the social worker still here and does she have the guardianship papers?"

Rudy escorts a Hispanic lady with a badge that says Leona Martinez. "Mrs. Martinez, am I to understand there is no one here to take the children?"

"Not here…Captain Hampton," Mrs. Martinez hands Pam the clip board for the temporary guardianship of Romy and Leo. I sign them next and then she says, "The State of Illinois thanks you for doing this. Have we located any surviving family members?"

"According to ICE agents here, all the children were sold to these Russians. The only ones, who don't have any family living that can take them, are the Drivas children." Rudy sadly remarks on how Romy and Leo were abandoned by their mother's parents; fanatical cult leaders named Cyrus and Margie Williams of Fayetteville, Arkansas. "Apparently, from what Arkansas officials told the agents in Fayetteville, Williams' followers went out and found every relative of Michael Drivas and slaughtered them. Mrs. Martinez, I'd trust Captain Hampton; from all her former supervisors, she's good with children and knows how to gain their trust to their benefit."

Since the conversation with Mrs. Martinez continues, the kids move over to an ambulance where they receive a field evaluation from paramedics. "We have a slight problem," the female medic looks over at Pam. The kids have lice."

"Okay, what's the procedure in this case?" Pam asks and the paramedic gives her the evil eye. "I'm a cop not a mother; protocols differ from state to state and region to region. I ask because I am that clueless, okay?"

"Hospitals are very paranoid around here concerning social diseases. The kids are treatable, but it's like a literal prison decontamination procedure."

Pam considers the medic's words and looks to Rudy. "Call Uncle Gino and tell him as well as Aunt Toula I'm bringing them some special cases for hair."

After some sanitizing haircuts, showers and some fresh clothes with flip-flops, Romy and Leo looked like a pair of kids on summer vacation. However, Romy told Gino she wanted to look like actress Demi Moore in *G.I. Jane!* Leo liked his slick do and smiled when he put on his Ocean Pacific t-shirt with long denim shorts and flip-flops.

After the kids dressed, Pam sits with Romy and places a set of emerald earrings on each of the young girl's earlobes. "Wow, where did you get these pretty earrings?"

Pam smiles as they peer into a mirror. "My mother gave me these earrings when I was about your age. I thought the earrings were very pretty too. Now, missy…let's go get some food in you and your brother."

Leo and I appear after the girls get ready and we drive over to the restaurant on West Belmont. Gus greets us and shows us to a table. He pulls Pam to the side. "What's with the kids and the haircuts?"

"They were sold into human trafficking by their maternal grandparents because they're freaky radical cultists. The kids had lice, dirty clothes and didn't eat for almost twelve hours. Parents and father's Greek relatives; all slaughtered by these cult people. Joe and I took them because the state had no resources to place them."

"So, what's the cover story in case your mother asks?"

"The bald heads symbolized programming by cult leaders, and we rescued them before the nut jobs completed the task." Pam smiles.

Then Leo offers a thought; another country heard from. "We say it like this Mr. Gus; that's our story and we're sticking to it!"

"Wise words," Gus says as he walks passed Pam. "I'm surprised they are this well-behaved. I expected more wise-cracks given their situation."

"The day's only half-way over Pop," Pam playfully cautions as Gus laughs. Then Maria walks in and I shake with anticipation. "Children, this is Mrs. Maria and she co-owns the restaurant with Mr. Gus."

"Hello Mrs. Maria," Leo smiles.

"Hi Mrs. Maria; nice to meet you." Romy also smiles as Pam nods to her. "My name is Andromeda and that's my younger brother Leonidas."

"I'm pleased to meet both of you. Why are your heads…bald?"

"If I may Pam?" Pam nods to Romy. "My mom's parents…are leaders of a crazy, fanatical cult. Our dad was Greek; his last name was Drivas. Our maternal grandparents killed everyone Greek we ever loved, and then tried to turn us into crazy versions of them. We rebelled and were sold to the Russians. Joe and Pam rescued us and the bald heads…was due to the crazy cult conditioning our crazy grandparents trying to turn Leo and me into…Hitler youth!"

"Hitler…youth?" Maria asks as if someone's trying to con her. I know my mother-in-law is a smart woman and can tell when family members hide things from her, but for some reason, she doesn't call Romy on her claim. "That sounds…horrible. And Child Services asked you and Joe to take them?"

"Yes, it's possible with their testimony, to shut down child trafficking of this type. So, Romy and Leo are material witnesses."

"Well, I certainly buy that over the *Hitler Youth* guff I was fed a moment ago," Pam snickers as Romy shakes her head. "Now, what's the truth behind your lack of hair my dear?"

Pam looks at Romy to say this is her show, so the young lady continues, "Okay, okay you caught me Mrs. Maria; the truth is…we had a serious infestation of lice. Pam took us over to your other brother Gino and he gave us our new dos. Then we showered and got this new wardrobe. That's how we ended up here."

Maria listens and watches Pam as she sees Romy look to her for confidence. "Trust is a fragile thing…Andromeda. What has Pam done…to gain your trust?" Romy starts to cry; Maria realizes Pam's done much for this girl.

"She helped me with my bath; listened to me, hugged me when I started…talking about my evil grandfather. He, he touched me…between my legs…I hate him!"

Maria looks into Pam's angry eyes and remembers the day she told Maria of Charles Dupree Junior's abuses. And when a child suffers the same kind of treatment, Maria knows Pam's protective nature as a cop, is as vicious as any Greek mother. "This girl and her brother; this is more than arresting these Russians…this part of the case, angers you more than yesterday."

"And you know why…Mom," Pam says quietly. "It's also, a painful reminder of what Charlie…prevented me from doing."

"And that is…?" Pam's sad eyes confirm Maria's worst fear as Pam nods. "Oh…my poor baby!" Maria's tears overflow as she embraces Pam. The children stand and walk over to me.

Leo looks into my eyes and asks, "What's wrong with Pam?"

I look over and Pam nods. I guess since she just told her mother, the one person who would fuss the most, the kids need to know the reason for her tears. "Before we came to Chicago, Pam met with two doctors who help women give birth to babies. Both doctors told Pam, she can't give birth to babies. That's why she and her mom are so sad."

When brother and sister look at one another, I can almost tell what they're thinking. My question is, would Pam and I be able to handle it? And in my honest opinion, which might be slightly skewed because the kids are so doggone cute; I think we can handle it!

Ten

CPD calls and tells Pam there is no available office space for her use. Luckily for her, Gus keeps an alcove office for overflow paperwork for his restaurant chain. Pam sets up her laptop and taps into the CPD information network. I set my laptop up to check on the education level of Romy and Leo.

I watch as each child plays the language, math and science computer games designed for learning. I notice each one, both Romy and Leo, scored high on certain levels of achievement. *Well, maybe education experts shouldn't discount home schooling as a viable alternative to public education. Then again, public school helped me!* Of course these random thoughts in my head certainly do nothing to prove or disprove this idea one way or another. However, I do have a clear understanding what to do when the subject of public education comes up when Pam and I do have children in some shape or form. "Joe, look at this!" I see Leo's smile as his talent for the artistic takes my breath away. I see his computer rendition of a World War II Dreadnought class Battleship *Texas*. "Do you like it?"

"Wow Leo, I am impressed buddy. Pam, I believe we have an artist in this fellow."

"I saw that, but you need to taste this!" Pam holds a spoon with her hand and in the spoon sits a tasty morsel from Gus's restaurant kitchen. The roast lamb bits taste fantastic with spices of oregano, garlic and even a little black pepper. "So, you think my dad should hire this cook?"

"If he doesn't, he's nuts for letting this cook go!" Then Romy stands up and grins. "You cooked this tender bit of lamb?"

"I did, and he asked me to call him 'Grandpa' Gus…why?" Romy asks with confusion in her eyes.

"Is it okay to hug the pretty bald Greek girl who just cooked some delicious lamb?"

Romy smiles and nods as embrace her as if she were my daughter. "I think Gus wanted you to call him 'Grandpa' Gus, because you are close to the age of many of his grandchildren. And, I think he also wanted to show you…not all grandfathers are like Cyrus Williams."

"Funny thing is Joe; I know…'Grandpa' Gus isn't like him at all. I mean he's like Dad when Dad was alive; we'd cook together, experiment different recipes we threw together and then wrote down later." I let go as Romy gets up and sits down next to Pam. "Did your family ever do that Pam?"

"We did and there are times I miss those moments Romy. I don't regret becoming a Marine or a cop, but I would trade one hour of those moments, for two hours of cooking and enjoying those moments when I was a kid." Then Pam looks into the smile of Romy. "Why do you ask Romy?"

I watch as tears fall from Romy's eyes as well as Leo's. "Leo and I think…we'd like you guys to be our parents." Wow, sweet little Romy, speaks what is in Pam's heart and mine. "We know, it would take time for everything to work out, but we'd wait."

"Well, at least you guys understand; this is an uphill battle from here." I didn't sugarcoat the challenge because it would be a challenge. Not so much for Pam and I, we have Romy and Leo's love and trust. The challenge will be for the prospective grandparents; on both sides. The hurt both children endure now, is the challenge they must overcome. "Something it took me a long time to learn, is when someone in my family hurt me badly, I had to learn to forgive them. I know it seems impossible, but forgiving someone who wronged and hurt you badly, like the Williams' did, forgiving them…frees you of them."

"You mean, all that stuff Mom and Dad said about forgiveness, before Grandpa Cyrus killed them, they meant it?" Leo's unbelief is understandable. But it is important for Romy and Leo that God will avenge them, and they need to leave the vengeance to Him.

Then Jason and Jennifer walked inside. Both wear denim slacks with different colored tops and black boots.

Jennifer smiles and slowly inches up behind Leo. "Joe, Pam; Jason and I heard you two are looking after a pair of cute kiddos. And I see in front of me, this one looks like a mini-Marine!"

"Well, Ms. Jennifer, what do you think of the *G.I. Jane* look-alike with the pretty emerald earrings?" Pam asks as her phone rings. "Hampton, yes Sal? I see, not only the pushers, but you found the lab; that's awesome." A few more moment talking to Sal and then Pam hangs up. "Step two: Krontzky's entire drug operation just went down an hour ago."

"What was in the lab?" Jennifer asks as Leo reaches up and hugs her. "Wow, and I get a hug from a mini-Marine!"

"Easy does it buddy; that lady's spoken for, okay?" Pam smiles at Leo then continues. "Intelligence Unit and three other districts closed in on the drug operation being run from a warehouse near Wrigley Field. It was a joint-op with the drug unit of the FBI, CPD and DEA. We have pushers, cooks, wholesale suppliers; the works! DEA and FBI get to share credit for this monstrous bust and we get fifteen minutes of face time with the soldiers to paint the next link in the chain. About ten million in drugs and equipment."

"Hey Pam," Rudy walks in as he sees the kids bald. He smiles, "Let me guess, the movie *1984?*"

"No, Leo thought it was a cool do and Romy wanted to look like Demi Moore from *G.I. Jane*," Pam smiles and then she nods. "What else do you have for me Rudy?"

Rudy smiles. "The rest of the family made me the liaison to you by proxy; so all my info is what you get from the field. Argyle, Thea's father-in-law over at BOC (Bureau of Organized Crime), informed me they traced four businesses owned by these families. They have a bank, brothel, dry cleaner, and the spa. My task force with the FBI is serving federal search warrants as well as the FISA with the Russian FSB angle. We're calling in VICE to handle the brothel and the Treasury Dept. to handle the bank."

Pam looks at me and smiles her evil little grin all Greek women smile when God smiles on them with good karma.

"Joe, Vaughns, Uncle Rudy; it's time for me to go pick a fight!" Then Romy and Leo run up and grab Pam in big bear hugs. "Hey, what's all this fuss about guys?"

"We don't want you to go!" Leo's anxiety and tears force Pam to delay her intentions. And for that matter, Romy joins him with the pleas.

"Pam, these guys are killers and they aren't human. In our group of kids from Arkansas, we had thirty of us. When we finally got here, there were only twelve, me and Leo included."

"Romy," Pam looks into the girl's eyes and smiles. "I'm gonna be okay baby; you know why?" Romy shakes her head as she hugs both children. "I'm not going alone; I have my own mob of cops. Joe and Uncle Jason will provide cover for me. Aunt Jen will stay here and look after you and Leo for me. She has kids of her own, so she knows how to protect kids. And she's vicious in her scheme."

Jennifer gives a little growl as Leo rolls his eyes. "I've been known to be quite…protective when someone's been hurt like you two. I'm a mom that means I'm as or even more protective than Pam is right now. But something you guys need to know; she's one of my cops who loves her job as well. And she needs to work this…so she can end this, come back here, and talk to you two about the adoption process. The Greeks call guts…faros. And you have to have faros like Pam to get this job done!"

Romy sighs heavily, "I'm sorry Aunt Jennifer; Leo and me; we're a little short on faros at the moment."

"When you need your guts and even more courage, is when you appear in court to testify against your grandparents and these Russian dirt bags. While Pam goes and deals with these guys, I'll be here looking after you. So, you want to see Pam disappear and reappear…maybe an hour or two later?"

"How?" Leo asks innocently. Romy looks at Jennifer with confusion in her eyes as well.

Jennifer extends her arms out. "You guys hug me like you did Pam.

"And we'll see what happens." Both kids grab on to Jennifer as Pam slips out the door and I follow. But before we make a clean get away, Jennifer yells, "Ala kazam!"

The afternoon brings a new form of entertainment as four police districts descend on the Red Square Spa. Pam's in her CPD vest with Uncles Sal, Rudy, and her in-law Argyle also in riot gear and walk into the spa. Jason at one end of the roof and me at the other with both of us with our sniper weapon of choice. We listen in on the conversation. *"Well, well Kostas…look at what we have here, the finest of Chicago Police Department serving warrants. You have nothing at all!"*

I hear Pam stoke the fire. *"Alexi Krontzky, Asst. Chief Superintendent Pamela Hampton; we are serving search warrants for: prostitution, illegal gambling, narcotics trafficking, human trafficking and commission of a terrorist act on US soil. Oh, and you won't be seeing Tatyana Brezhnev for a while. The last team she was with, ended up either dead or in custody. Seems kidnapping by foreign agents under FISA, constitutes a violation of the U.S. Patriot Act. She's headed to GITMO as we speak."*

I could hear the quiet rage of Krontzky's voice. *"She has rights!"*

"The people she killed in Corpus Christi, here in Chicago; they had rights too…because they are citizens of this country and were born with them! So, if you wish to complain that we're violating your rights by serving legal court documents, please call your lawyer or your consulate in New York; you'll find little or no sympathy I'm afraid."

Pam's second volley gains the fateful question from Krontzky, *"What do you mean by* little or no sympathy *Superintendent Hampton?"*

She closes the *shock and awe* portion of picking this fight. *"As I look at my watch, yes…as of twenty-four hours ago Moscow time, all three heads of your families here, ceased to exist.*

Jim E. Johnson

"With the assistance of President Putin's office and Russian observers, a crack commando unit infiltrated the territory around Strelka, Siberia; and laid waste to every home, business and those who lived and worked named Krontzky, Kirov, or Brezhnev. The Russian FSB never authorized those deaths and no one in the Russian parliament authorized the death of the late Western Deputy Trade Minister Yuri Rasputin Petrov. For commission of genocide against the Petrov family, your own government decreed you suffer the same fate. Also, if you haven't figured it out by now; no one connected to Miss Petrov knows where she is. Her mother was very careful to not leave a trail."

"We know," now I wasn't expecting that answer. *"The whole plan hinges on seeing all this wholesale death suffered by your officers, Chief Vaughn's officers and other federal agents, to bring them back so we can take possession of Miss Petrov. That is all that matters."*

Krontzky just confesses to multiple capital offenses of murder, kidnapping and acts of terror, and he sounds cool as a cucumber? Something about this isn't right. "Cowboy to Goddess; watch your six…repeat, watch your six!" I look over at Jason. "Cover me; I'm going in after her!" As I cross the street, I hear gun shots.

Then Jason yells, *"All units, all units; shots fired…move, move!"* I see out of the corner of my eye Jason shimmy down the fire escape and joins me on the ground. We run inside the spa and go past what appears to be an executive bar, all shot up with many of Krontzky's bodyguards down on the ground bleeding from gunshot wounds. Krontzky bailed out of the building.

When I turn to view the bath entrance, my horror etched as Rudy and Sal, huddle over my wounded wife. "Pam!"

"Before you get all bent out of shape and all protective Longhorn, it's just a flesh wound."

"Oh yeah, just a flesh wound she says," Sal smarts off as Pam gives him the evil eye. "Were you ever shot when you were an active-duty Marine?"

"Twice; once in Fallujah in my left shoulder. And once in Baghdad in the left ass cheek. Joe already knows about these old wounds of mine. The right shoulder's a new one." I shake my head as Jason snickers. Pam notices my face full of anxiety and my heavy sighs. "Joe, I'm okay."

"I know; I'll feel better when you get checked out." I never thought such concern would come from my voice; especially when Pam's work as a cop comes into play. I guess I'm now like every other spouse of a law enforcement officer; full of the same fears and worries all have with this job. "I'm sorry I sounded like a worrisome, overprotective spouse just now."

"If you didn't; I'd think something was wrong with you Longhorn," Pam smiles as paramedics arrive. "Okay kids, load me up and take me over to St. Mary's so I can get this shoulder repaired please?" The paramedics nod as I kiss Pam. She asks, "Joe?"

"Yes dear?" That's a question I'm used to asking these days.

"Tell Romy and Leo I'm okay? And I'm sorry Jen's magic trick won't work the reverse as it should."

"Don't count it out too quick. See you at St. Mary's?" Pam nods as I look to Jason. "Take Rudy and go get Jen and the kids and meet me at St. Mary's ER?"

"On my way," Jason taps Rudy in the arm and both leave.

I look at the paramedic who stays in the back with Pam. "Mind if I tag along?"

The paramedic, a young woman named Alice, nods to me. "Hop in; you can ride with us!" I nod as I hold Pam's hand and her smile relieves all my tension.

Eleven

"Pam!" Both Romy and Leo yell as they run up to Pam, only to be caught by me and Jason.

"Whoa guys; Pam has a shoulder wound so be careful, okay?" Both kids nod as they both walk up and take turns hugging Pam from their left side. "They were a little worried about you."

"Me, why worry about a tough broad like me?" Pam smiles impishly as the kids smile at her. "Okay, I get a bullet hole in the right shoulder...I'm not so tough."

Romy pouts; that's the first time I've seen that girl show any kind of negative emotion toward us. "That's not funny at all Pam. We were scared to death!"

"Wow, oh ye of little faith! Romy, I wasn't going to die, because I had plenty of backup sweetie. Getting shot is scary; I'll admit that. And the moment that bullet hit me, I felt like someone killed me. Then the shock wore off and all I had was a shoulder wound." Pam looks to me and I mouth to her *she really is scared!* Pam nods and hugs Romy again, "I'm sorry Romy; I won't joke like that around you or your brother again."

"Thank you, Pam," Leo goes over and hugs her as an ER doctor completes stitching Pam's wound. Leo asks, "Is Pam gonna be okay Doc?"

The gray-haired doctor with blue eyes and round glasses smiles at Leo. "She will be fine young man. The bullet went clean through, but she'll need looking after for a day or two. You think you and your sister can help with that?"

"I bet we can...with Joe's help of course," Romy smiles as do I. And she's right; all three of us can and will help Pam get better.

The scary part: when Gus and Maria bust into the ER. "Pamela, are you trying to give your father and me heart attacks? I knew you went to confront those Russian monsters, but get yourself shot?"

"Well Ma, that's why I live and work in Texas; less likely to be shot since I spend most of my time in an office," Pam says as the kids keep close to her. "And according to the doctor, I need to rest for a day or two."

"We'll stay with them over at Mike and Thea's place," Jennifer volunteers she and Jason to help out as Maria glares at Jennifer. Jennifer sighs, "You really think that killer look in your eyes scares me in the least Maria? I hate you burst your bubble, but it doesn't. So I'll give you two minutes to yell, fret, or whatever you hate about me…out of your system…go!"

Jennifer glances at her watch as Maria's shock engulfs the moment. Then Pam's mother finds her voice. "You, you are treated like a blood relative when you are not. I don't hate you for this Jennifer; I simply do not understand why my daughter would choose that over her own blood."

"Instead of asking Jennifer, why didn't you ever ask me…Ma?" Pam's eyes well with tears and as they flow, Maria's eyes flow with tears as well. "You know why I chose a surrogate family over my own? How about how you and Dad spoke of not polluting our family line with outsiders. Your very words and attitudes smack of supremacy and hypocrisy. At the very core…racist. You said yesterday…you had ungrateful daughters. Did Thea…disgrace you somehow by marrying a man and having a family? I'd think you were happy she gave you handsome grandsons." Pam takes a breath; then she concludes her thoughts. "So tell me Ma, do you hate those of your children…who stepped outside the community?"

"That's not what I said Pamela…" Maria paces then lets loose. "Why couldn't you just trust us to look out for you? Why did you move to Virginia; move in with my sister, become a Marine? I don't understand these things about you!"

"You never did," Pam says quietly as she nods to me. "Would all of you excuse us please?" I take the kids in hand as Jason and Jennifer escort Gus from the ER exam room.

We all walk to the waiting room so Pam and Maria could finally hash this, whatever it is out.

After almost an hour of watching news programs and watching Leo amuse himself with the learning games on the waiting room computer, Maria and Pam come out with Pam's right arm in a sling. "Do you need me to go by the drug store to pick up your medication?"

"Ma, the drugstore is on the way to Thea's apartment. They will have the prescription filled by the time I get there." Then both Jennifer and I give Pam one of those *she's your mother* corrective gazes. "Before I let you drive me to the drugstore and back to Thea's place, you have to promise me something Ma."

"Anything darling," Maria smiles as Gus shakes his head. "What?"

"Ma, you have to promise me...no side trips; straight to the drugstore and then straight to Thea's."

"Oh darling," when Pam holds up her forefinger, Maria relents. "All right, drugstore; then to Thea's."

Jason, Jennifer, the kids, and I wait for Pam and Maria at Thea's apartment. "According to the distance and the time to reach the drugstore, Maria and Pam should be here any moment." I say that, but if I were a gambling man, I'd bet Maria breaks her promise and takes a few side trips. But to my pleasant surprise, I'm wrong. Maria arrives with Pam in tow. "Welcome ladies."

"Bah!" Maria snorts as Pam smiles like a crooked leprechaun. "I tried to take her by the restaurant, and she pulled a gun on me!" Maria glares at Pam, "Ungrateful child!"

I smile as well. "Well Maria, you did promise to take her straight to the drugstore and then here to Thea's place. I believe she worked from the old adage, *beware of Greeks bearing gifts!* So you're volunteering to take her on her rounds I have to ask myself; why the side trip to the restaurant?"

Maria's answer shocks everyone, "A prominent family from Athens…wants Pamela…to marry one of their sons."

"What?" Pam's ire just hit the moon and bounces back immediately. "I am married Mother! How dare you to presume to speak for me when I am already married?"

"You call being married to him…a proper marriage? I am sorely disappointed in you! It was bad enough your sister married Michael; then you had to go off and marry Joe? Did you learn nothing from your mistake to Charles Dupree?"

"I am sick and tired of you…trying to change my life to suit your own perceived notions!" Pam dials her cell phone and gets Gus. "Dad, is there some family from Athens expecting me?"

"Your mother said you wanted to meet them…what's wrong?"

"Dad," Pam's so frustrated she wants to shoot Maria. Instead, she outs Maria to Gus. "Mom lied to you. I never even knew about these people visiting from Athens. She just tried to arrange a new marriage behind mine and Joe's backs. And right now, I am too damned angry to care about her motives or the end result. Please bring an extra person and come pick her up and her car."

A few minutes later, Gus and Sal arrive, and Sal's expression is less than friendly. "What have you done to your mother?" Sal asks as Pam's rage pushes her off the sofa and into Sal's face.

"What I did, was make sure she understood the consequences of her continued misbehavior; a fact I thought you learned earlier this morning! I'm having difficulty trying to do my job when the family I'm trying to protect, is going against everything I'm trying to accomplish! Uncle Sal, why did she send for a Greek family from Athens to arrange another marriage for me when I am already married? What kind of sense does that make?"

"It makes no sense," Sal's voice echoes the concern now. Maria turns and sees the displeasure in her brother's eyes and looks to Gus for support. His reveal the same displeasure and now she understands. Pam is not the problem, she is.

"If you will not listen to your daughter, or your husband, listen to me…leave Pamela to do her job! And as far as Joe is concerned, you leave that alone too!" Maria's indignant expression precedes a scoff as she storms out of the apartment. Sal turns to Pam, "I'm sorry about that. I think her condition, whatever it is, is worsening."

"I suggest you and Pop take her and get her checked out before I shoot her; making my father a widower and you…one sister less." Pam shakes her head as Romy whispers to and hugs her. "That sounds delicious."

"Romy need help?" Gus asks smiling.

"I got this Gus; you handle Maria please?" I tell him as he and Sal leave. I look over at Romy, "So, what are we cooking this evening?"

"Lemon chicken; Aunt Jennifer and I stopped by the butcher shop down the street to get everything." Jennifer smiles as she hands a glass of iced tea to Pam. "Pam, go ahead and get comfortable. I can get Joe and Uncle Jason to help out."

"I'll go sit at the table and get Aunt Jen to help me then," Pam smiles as she kisses Romy on the cheek and goes to sit down. Once seated, Jennifer sets Pam's laptop up. "Looks like primo office space at Pop's restaurant is out. Hey Joe, you heard from Thea?"

"I need to check in," I call Uncle Jake, "How's the family?"

"*All the families are great! You should see Liam and Sean; those boys are natural cowboys!*"

"Sounds like they're having a ball! I need to speak with John if he's there."

Uncle Jake passes off the phone to my little brother John. "*Hey bro, what's up?*"

"Anybody tail you guys from Love Field to Denton at all?"

"*Picked up two black Mercedes SUVs with Russian Diplomatic plates. I called in a favor with the local Texas Ranger office. The…couriers, as they called themselves, were detained for questioning until Washington called and requested, they be released.*"

"Tell me you used the old, unmarked car your lieutenant loaned you?"

"Oh I did, and Uncle Jake and Cody had an old Bronco sitting in a parking spot with an updated registration. Look, we were careful and if someone no one knows appears in Denton, the whole town knows, and it gets to the ranch. Plus, unless the Russians are specializing in Texas drawls, we'll have these kids cold!"

"Don't get cocky Little Brother and watch your six!" I hang up as Pam stares at me. "Everyone is okay. Liam and Sean are helping with the ranch chores and according to Uncle Jake; they're real cowboys!"

Pam laughs, "So the boys are really into it huh?"

"Yeah and I just received a text from Mike; apparently Thea's working on her tan."

"Wait," Pam gives me one of those *I'm shocked* looks. "I don't remember her packing a bathing suit."

I couldn't contain my laughter. I mean, Pam's sister is a tall, beautiful brunette. And she has a runway model body, with some well-placed extra padding in the right places. But she and Mike are well-matched. "Aunt Wanda had suits of all shapes, sizes and styles. I'm sure she found one that fit."

"Ew, would you use a previously worn swimsuit?" Romy asks as Pam joins her in having the willies.

Jennifer offers a thought, "I'd say over half those suits Wanda never wore. I'm sure Jake threw out all her old clothes?"

"He did; including all the swimsuits she always wore at different times...Thea's safe."

Pam wipes sweat drops away, "Thank God!"

I laugh as I season the chicken with a black pepper rub Jason once taught me to make in Bosnia. You take a pinch of salt, three pinches of black pepper; add lemon juice and a little garlic powder and the rub cooks into the chicken for a fresh, lemon taste...with a garlic kick. Romy and Leo walk up, "Is the chicken ready to bake?"

"Yes ma'am; put it in at 375° for an hour and it should be nice and tasty. You guys getting the sides together?"

"Oh, I'm helping with that Joe," Jennifer smiles as she pulls out a can of mixed vegetables. "Remind me what we cook so I can replace it from the market."

"Jen, I called Thea moments ago, she told me to just leave some cash in the cigar box on top of the bread box. Probably what we're cooking, her family will never touch. She said thanks for looking out for me."

"Hey, when we're not here, I'm your boss as well as your friend; it's my job to look out for you." Then I watch Pam sigh as Jennifer picks up on that tick as well. "Okay, what's wrong?"

Jason and I take over the cooking chores as the kids roll into the dining area to hug Pam. "Oh you guys are sweet; thanks for the cuddles." Each kisses her on a cheek and they return to the kitchen. Pam resumes her conversation. "Between Ma and Thea; it's like night and day on relationships. Ma acts like some deranged older sister who can't get her act together while Thea…acts like the mother I need. How did the roles get so reversed?"

"Maybe…your mother does have dementia. And Thea knows you need support from your family to protect and serve your family. She knows you want to be loved for you and not your mother's crazy version of you. Something in your relationship with Maria…snapped a long time ago. And until you both deal with it; you'll never heal from it."

I could see the wheels turning in Pam's mind as if she searched a database for the right video to replay. It's like a veteran suffering from PTSD (Post Traumatic Stress Disorder); the right video gives you the right information needed to deal with a situation. In Pam's case, it's a memory her mother shares, that might have scared Maria beyond reason. And I fear the memory involves Charles Dupree Junior!

Twelve

The lemon chicken fills our bellies with satisfaction. And since the kids helped significantly with cooking dinner, Jason and I wash up the dishes as well as the cookware. Thea's gonna love the cooked lemon smell of her kitchen. When Jason and I complete our labors, we join our girls and the kids as Pam tells how she and the Harvard Sorority Sisters met. "…when Aunt Ruthie walked up to the front desk, she surveyed four young women, close to my age, and asked how they would pay for their rooms. Well, Jennifer breaks out the explanation concerning their hotel reservations getting all screwed up. And that all their money was blown trying to correct the oversight which they were treated rudely by the manager and the front desk. Now, I'm not one to usually pull Aunt Ruthie to the side about rooms, but I did point out no one made reservations and we could use the occupancy. I told her she could take what they could afford, and I'd pay the balance from my paychecks. So Aunt Ruthie took a dollar from each and then my aunt was surprised when the girls rose early and we, the five of us, cooked breakfast and cleaned the beach house for the next round of customers."

Romy and Leo's eyes widen as Romy asks, "What happened the next day?"

Jennifer smiles; meaning she has the other half of the story. "I called my father who got it all straightened out and he came over later and paid the balance of our stay and Ruthie's. He thanked her generously for her willingness to put up with an awkward situation. Sometime later that day, we all met Jason and his friends. Joe was still deployed in Bosnia and none of us had met him yet."

"And those stories are not for consumption where young people younger than eighteen are concerned." Jason nods to me and I nod back. I see Romy and Leo look at us like we grew a third eye on our foreheads. It never fails.

Jennifer and Pam giggle as Pam gets a call on her cell phone. "Hampton, talk to me. Yes Rudy, what is it?"

Rudy's voice holds great concern; especially when the concern involves material witnesses. *"You're not going to believe this, but Cyrus and Margie Williams are here for Andromeda and Leonidas."*

Pam hears Cyrus yell in the background, *"Their names are Andrea and Leon; not those…damned foreign names my daughter gave them!"*

"Oh boy; he sounds a little…xenophobic to me!" Pam shakes her head. "How in the hell did those two get past all the law enforcement nets out of Arkansas?"

"I don't know; but they are here at the 18th District to claim the children. Child Services insists you hand them over. Unless…you have an order of protection."

"Mike filed an order of protection against the Williams' prior to their sudden departure. Joe and I will meet you and them there in an hour."

Pam and I arrive at the 18th District as Cyrus Williams rages like a wounded mountain lion. "I want to see my grandchildren! My wife and I are their legal guardians and we demand they be returned to us now!" Pam and I walk up as the old man with a white-hair comb-over and dark, brown eyes walks up. His white-bearded chin hid the gritting teeth behind his lips. A faded denim shirt with faded jeans completed his salt-of-the-earth motif and he spoke quietly. "Pardon me ma'am, do you know where I can find my grandchildren?" He hands pictures of Romy and Leo to the desk sergeant as well as Rudy. "We thought they were going to summer camp but were abducted and brought here."

Pam looks at the photos and back to Williams and asks again, "And what were their names again Mister…?"

"Williams, Cyrus Williams of the Lord's Light Brigade Church of Fayetteville, Arkansas. My wife Margie and I shepherd that flock of believers.

"The children's names are Andrea and Leon. And who might you be ma'am?"

Pam turns to Rudy who gives her a goofy grin. She returns it and turns back to face Williams. "I am Acting Asst. Chief Sup. Int. Pamela Hampton. These children you claim are your grandchildren; were rescued as part of a human trafficking sting we netted twelve children who were victimized by the Russian mob. I'm afraid they are being held as material witnesses as part of that investigation."

"That's absurd," says Margie Williams, a woman with cold blue eyes and faded blonde hair. The scary part: she reminds me of my Aunt Wanda! "What did the little heathens say about us?"

"Such a hateful thing to say about a pair of well-behaved children," I say that knowing they can be imps at times. But why spoil the moment since both Williams' are fit to be tied. "Let me tell you what you did in this case already Mr. and Mrs. Williams. We found them dirty from head to toe. Malnourished, holes in their shoes and clothing, hair full of lice and then we found their legal names on a list of kids and guess where they were being sent?" I could see the tension in their faces increase as I continued to describe the children's once deteriorating condition. "These were about to be sent, undocumented I might add, to Turkey…and their paternal heritage is Greek!"

"In addition to that; Child Protective Services placed with them us and also…sprung for a Federal Order of Protection against one Cyrus Williams and one Margie Williams of Fayetteville, Arkansas on behalf of Andromeda Christina and Leonidas Timothy Drivas. Furthermore, this order bars contact with the children for up to one hundred feet based on their appearance upon arrival here in Chicago." When Pam's on a roll, I let her roll. "There have been…allegations made against Mr. Cyrus Williams by Andromeda for inappropriate touching of her body." Then she stops and asks, "Has this couple been read their rights?"

"They have," Rudy says with a smile. I could see both of the grandparents fidget like they have nervous conditions.

I believe they know we have them.

"Now," Pam let's her oozy new southern drawl ease out as she looks directly into Cyrus Williams' eyes. "Would you care to revise your story…Mr. Williams?"

Both look at one another and Williams belts out, "We…want a lawyer."

Pam motions uniform patrol officers to cuff both the Williams', "Mr. and Mrs. Williams; you are under arrest for child endangerment, reckless abandonment and human trafficking. Take them away Officer Kapelos." As both are cuffed and led away, Pam turns to us and smiles. "If they hate Greeks so much, they can be arrested by Greek cops!"

"Wow that sounds like profiling to me!" We turn to find another beauty with flaxen hair and gorgeous brown eyes. Her summer dress denoted her supermodel frame as ACLU attorney Florentine Gardelli walks inside the lobby. "What's up guys?"

"Oh hell Flora, what are you doing here?"

Flora hugs Pam and Pam winces a bit. "Sorry, how's the arm?"

"It's my shoulder and it hurts like the dickens. I went to serve warrants and arrest some heads of local Russian crime families when I was shot."

"One of them did that?" Flora asks with surprise in her voice.

"Yeah and here's the kicker: this guy used to be Russian FSB," Pam responds with sarcasm in her voice as Flora laughs. "Anyway, no word on him since he and another guy escaped. And I believe the other guy is this specimen." Pam shows Flora a photo of Marko Kirov. "So, whatcha think Sister Flora?"

"Good-looking guy; but I hate the taste of vodka. Nope, he's a loser from the word go."

"His name he used to impersonate a Marine was Marcus Shaw; mother's maiden name and he moved to Russia when he was sixteen after she died." Pam just shakes her head. "Jason and TFCC exposed this knucklehead. And as soon as we find him, I'm turning TFCC agents present here…loose on this clown."

"Yeah…about that," Flora says and now we have the reason why she might be here. "Annie…wanted me to get an update for…DMD on this case."

"Tell her she's too late; already have federal agencies in on it. And they know about…DMD's under-the-table deal with the FSB to protect their business interests." Pam drops that bomb and Flora nods repentantly. "Right now, I'm under Title Eighteen to not discuss this case unless it is part of our inner city task force with the feds."

"How did you get command?"

"Appointment by Chief Superintendent Brown, with approval by the FBI as well as DEA, ICE and NCIS." I believe Pam is allowed to tell Flora that much under Title Eighteen. "By the way, did Dominique ever send sympathy cards to the three families of the uniformed cops CCPD lost due to these Russians shooting up Corpus Christi like the O.K. Corral?"

"You're actually…hanging all that on her?"

"Yes, I am, and she knows why. So, unless you're here about another case; I've said all I can say." Then Flora points her thumb to where the newly arrested grandparents went. "Are you kidding me?"

"I wish I were," Flora shakes her head as does Pam. "Legal Aid in Arkansas called Annie's office and asked if she or an associate could come here to check on the Lord's Light Brigade Church's involvement of the Drivas kids."

I could see Pam about to become unnerved. I step in. "Flora, did the church inform you and Annie they attempted to change the names of the kids; which the kids rejected?"

Flora's confusion comes to the forefront. "I was told; the children accepted their new names."

"Who…confirmed that information?" And I ask because the kids I've shared two meals with already didn't indicate that.

"An Uncle…Jasper Williams did," Flora informs us the church or cult is rallying behind Cyrus and Margie.

"Why, what have you learned?"

"We caught them lying a few minutes ago. The girl accused old man Cyrus of inappropriate touching of her person. And if this kid's acting, she deserves an Emmy for her performance. But Flora, every fiber in my being, tells me she's been molested and the scars on the boy's back were not due to some simple issue of disobedience. Added to the fact, they witnessed their parents taken away and come to find out they were murdered…you put it together for me." Flora Gardelli's a smart woman. I can't believe she or Annie Wells would fall for a cult's assertions these kids wanted to be there or here. "Anyway, Child Protective Services awarded guardianship to a couple because they are material witnesses in their own human trafficking case. They, along with ten other children were sold to these Russians to leave the U.S."

"You know the couple; don't you Joe?" Damn, she's good. But I dare not say another word.

Pam rescues me, "It's us Flora and no; you may not know their location. But out of respect for your case, or potential case, we will choose a safe, neutral site where you can speak with them with someone, they trust…present."

"Who is neutral enough?"

"Jason or Jennifer Vaughn," Pam looks deep into Flora's eyes and shakes her head. "It's them or you go home."

"That bad?"

"These kids…are that scared Flora." Pam makes no bones about Romy and Leo's anxiety. "Something else you need to know; I would have asked my sister to represent the kids, but she's in hiding to protect her family from these Russians. So, if you can get Annie Wells on board, they can use an advocate in their corner besides us and the Vaughns."

"I'll call her!" After fifteen minutes of Flora being on the phone, I could see she's in a heated discussion with her partner. After another few minutes, Flora hangs up and gives us a dejected head shake. "No go; Annie wants no part of it."

"Then tell her; you speaking with the children…is a no go. As their guardians, we can't afford the risk to them. And tell Annie next time you speak with her; inform her Jennifer will be calling Dominique. And have her tell Dominique; be prepared for an obstruction to a federal investigation charge…promise!" Yes, I am officially this angry. So I call Jason. "Hey, how are the little darlings?"

"We're all doing great. Thea and her family are back. They met Romy and Leo and adore them. Joe, Thea informed us she is volunteering to be the children's advocate. So, what's with the call?"

"Flora Gardelli arrived to represent the interests of the Lord's Light Brigade Church, Cyrus Williams' church. Jace, if David and Dominique are involved…?"

"I will speak with them and remind them of their debt to me! And further action will place their freedom in severe jeopardy if they push this issue. Trust me, after the last three months, the last thing the Matthews family wants to do is piss me off."

"Fine, I'll tell Flora she's off the hook then. See you later," I hang up as Flora faces me, "Jason will speak with David and Dominique. I doubt they want to get involved in this any further."

"Good, one less thing I have to worry about," Pam joins us as if the pressure's off for now. "I'll let Rudy handle things here and…I want to go back to Thea's and see the kids."

"By the way, Thea and her family returned to a full house," I put it as mildly as possible. "And she thinks the kids are adorable."

"Then let's head back."

Thirteen

We return to Mike and Thea's place to see Thea and Jennifer baking desserts with Romy. "Wow, something smells delicious."

"Fresh Milopita and Baklava," Thea smiles as her new tan radiates the kitchen. "Joe; thanks for the hospitality. Your Uncle Jake loved having us at the ranch. Mike and the boys enjoyed helping out."

"Well Jake's started to enjoy visitors and for him, it's a good avenue to have the Stockton Ranch as a working dude ranch." Jake's, Mom's, and my discussions on this subject now bear fruit. I even footed the bills for Mike and Thea's trip. Uncle Jake was very grateful, and he had fun going along with it. Now, back to business. "Jason tells me you heard Romy and Leo's story?"

"Yes and I believe they need an advocate. I know a federal judge who can make the appointment. I'll call him and see if he can arrange the order. What do you have for me?"

Pam hands Thea a copy of the federal protection order. "Child Services and TFCC arranged this so we could serve as protective guardians in the interim. We went to Uncle Gino to help with getting them cleaned up."

"I see, is that why Leo looks like a mini-Marine and Romy's a Greek version of Sinead O'Connor?" Romy looks over at Thea and shakes her head. "Okay, O'Neil from *G.I. Jane*; but I agree with Pam…you make those earrings sparkle as well."

"Thank you; if it isn't too forward to call you…Aunt Thea? I'd feel silly calling you…*Thea* Thea."

"I'd feel silly if you called me that too! Regardless of whether it's out of affection or not; but I'm curious why you would call me *Aunt* or *Thea?*"

"Leo and I…wanted to try the title…out?"

"Just trying it out huh?" Thea gives Pam a suspicious glance as Pam winces like her shoulder hurts. "You, Acting Asst. Chief Super. Hampton; in my home office…please?"

I watch as Pam pouts like a little girl about to receive a scolding from her mother. "Aunt Thea?" Leo walks up and hugs Thea. "We just want Joe and Pam to adopt us, and we want to adopt them…as parents."

"Wait; that's what's going on here? You two and the kids, want to blend into a family?" Everyone nods as Thea turns to Pam, "Why didn't you just tell me Pam?"

"I didn't…want to get anyone's hopes up. And now I know how…vicious and wild these Russians are, I'm a little scared how all of this will turn out. Thea, I'm so, so scared."

Thea smiles and lightly touches the cheeks of not only Liam and Sean, but Romy and Leo as well. Then she put her arms around Pam. "Twelve hours ago, while we spent a short time on a ranch in Texas, you moved a case forward. You took in two adorable, yet scared kids when no one else could. You fed them, cleaned them up, and most importantly…you loved them like a mother should. And if that's the scariest thing you've done up till now, you're off to a fantastic start."

Pam laughs as she cries. I see Romy and Leo run up and she throws her arms around both of them. Of course her right shoulder slacks a bit due to the fire of pain shooting through it. "Easy, easy on the right shoulder; but I do love you guys very much."

"We love you too; so let's put that arm and shoulder back inside the sling," Romy smiles as she gently assists Pam put the sling back on. "There, now you can heal better."

"Thank you, and…what time is it?" Pam looks at her watch, "Oh my goodness, it is late, late, and late." I look at my watch. *9:30 pm might be time to go to bed.* "Aren't you two tired?"

"Now I'm getting tired," Leo leans against me like he's really pooped.

Pam has Romy leaning against her as she asks Thea. "How are you fixed on room with this crowd?"

"We use a proven method of handling multiple guests; guest ladies get the spare guest room, Leo can bunk down with one of the boys and Jason as well as Joe can take up the easy chair and the sofa." Sometimes, Thea's organizational skills remind me of Pam's. "Does that work?"

"Sounds like a solid plan," Jason smiles as he kisses Jennifer good night. I kiss Pam and Romy as she and Romy kiss me and Leo good night. Jason and I go and dress for the evening as we keep our side arms ready in case some idiot decides to storm through the front door.

The night passes without incident as Jason and I awake to the smell of sausage cooking in a frying pan and biscuits or some kind of breakfast pastry baking in the oven. "What's that I smell?" I ask as I get up from my perch.

"Cinnamon rolls, we thought they would be great with eggs and sausage," Thea smiles as Jason rises from his slumber. "Good morning Jace."

"Good morning Thea; my lady still in the shower?"

"Just got out; hiya handsome," Jennifer kisses Jason good morning. "Your turn in the shower."

"Thanks," Jason smiles as he walks down the hallway. I slip into a half-bath next to the living area as I change for my day. When I emerge, Jason's smiling at me. "Took your sweet time jarhead!"

"I took my time; how long was your shower?" Of course I'm a little put out by Jason's statement. But I remember watching Jason shave and bathe in the field. He cleans up nice and takes little time to do it. I hate that about him. "Anyway, I've been taking my time shaving so I don't cut myself. What's your excuse?"

"I like it when my husband's a little scruffy Joe. When he has a goatee, I find him twice as sexy." Jennifer smiles as Pam giggles. I lose an argument when I brag about my grooming or my quaff.

Pam walks up and kisses me. "Haven't you learned yet you're not ever winning that argument; he says that to tease you?"

"Oh I know; that's why I playfully call him squid once in a while!" Jason laughs as I do. I walk with Pam up to the kitchen table as the kids eat at the bar. "Thing is, he always played scruffy when he was in-country in Iraq when I was NCIS."

"And when it is a long case or something requires my whole attention, facial hair is the last thing on my mind," Jason smiles as does Romy.

"What are you smiling at kid?" Jennifer asks as Pam whispers in her ear. "Oh, is that why?"

"Excessive facial hair can be attractive to some." Pam smiles.

"Romy's only twelve; is she blooming early?" Jennifer's concern is real as is mine now. I wonder if my potential daughter is all she seems. I look at Pam and then both of us look to Romy. "Guys, everything okay?"

"Oh I'm sure it is Aunt Jen; but I want to make sure," Pam says as she sits down at the bar next to Romy. "When breakfast concludes; you, me and Aunt Jen are going for a walk. Joe, Uncle Jason and your brother will sit here to talk things over."

Romy quietly answers, "Yes ma'am." The look in her eyes is the same as yesterday when we met the kids for the first time.

Jason and I walk over by the front door to confer. "What do you make of that?"

Jason's profiling insights always blow my mind. "Think of a rubber band. Romy and Leo's circumstances once existed on an extreme stretch point. Now, the rubber band's snapping back. I fear it will take a lot longer for you two to break through to the truth. Maybe…there's some conditioning from the cult…that made its way into their souls."

"Okay…no walk, so we'll hash this out here." Something Jennifer and Pam see in Romy is scaring me. "Romy, what's going on with you?"

"Grandpa Cyrus…spent a lot of time with Romy Pam." Leo hides behind me as he speaks. "I know she bit his hands and nose. He slapped her so hard she bounced off the wall in her room."

"Shut up Leo!" Romy screams as Pam cautiously approaches Romy. "Why are you doing this Pam?"

"I need to know; how screwed up your pretty head is baby. I don't want to cause you pain. I want to help, but I need to know where your head is at Romy." Leo and I helplessly watch as Pam's attempts to call Romy's conditioning into question. Now Romy's tears flow like Niagara Falls as she shakes her head no. It's the first sign I've notice the cult's conditioning being inside Romy's head and heart. "Did Grandpa Cyrus do all this…damage to you?"

"No, Grandma Margie did too; and she tried to hurt Leo. That's why they're afraid of us…we fought back!" Slowly, like peeling an onion back, more of the truth unfolds. "We started hiding nails, kitchen knives, to fight back. Then one night, we went to sleep, and ending up coming here."

"Where did you learn to smile the smile you made to Uncle Jason?" Jennifer's question makes Romy smile again. "Yes, that smile."

"Mom always smiled at Dad like that." Now we get it; Romy's smile imitated the smiles and ticks her mother made when their parents were alive. She was learning courtship behavior from her parents.

"Romy, did your dad smile at your mom in the same way?" Jennifer asks as Romy nods. "The cult didn't teach her that; she learned it from her parents. She's learning how to be courted…by a boyfriend."

"She's only twelve Jen," Thea reminds every one of the pre-teen stage of Romy's growth. "Tell you what; we, meaning all the ladies, need to go shopping. We'll check and see if Sweet Romy's on her way to womanhood and if she is, we'll intervene with…the talk–the girl's version."

"And the guys will decompress by playing video games and talking guy…stuff," I shake my head as Mike attempts to hold up the male end of this ad hoc group. If nothing else, he did get his share of laughs from the ladies.

Just as the ladies start out the door, Pam receives a call from Uncle Rudy. "Hi Rudy, what's up?"

"We received something here at the 18th District I think you need to see."

"Why the secrecy?"

"You'll understand when you get here." Pam hangs up and shakes her head.

"What happened?"

Pam lightly shakes her head. "I dunno; Rudy said the 18th received some kind of delivery. He's pretty shook up. Rudy knows I'm supposed to rest due to getting shot, or he wouldn't ask me to come down there."

I'm starting to wonder since no one's been able to locate our Russian problem children if we're dealing with severed limbs or heads. Guess Pam and I will find out shortly. "I'll drive Pam while the rest go shopping. We might want to table…the talk, until Pam can be there for it."

"Are you sure?" Thea asks as Pam glares at her. "Okay, we'll wait."

"Thank you, sis; now, let's go Joe." We head out and fifteen minutes later, arrive at the 18th District. When we walk in, Rudy's wearing his signature denim slacks, a navy blue button-down shirt and white sneakers. "Okay, what's going on Rudy?"

"Follow me," we follow Rudy into an area where forensics experts are examining three boxes. "We received these early this morning; someone left them outside the delivery entrance."

When we look inside the boxes, Pam almost vomits on the spot. Inside the three boxes, holds the head of a missing local Russian mobster. The names: Alexi Krontzky, Tatyana Brezhnev, and our missing Marine wannabe…Marko Kirov.

Fourteen

We meet everyone at the Greek Town location of Papa Papadakis' Restaurant. And as if we need any more input, Gus and Maria appear; something we don't need is more input. "Anyone hungry?" Gus asks as he comes in wearing a grease-stained apron with a powder blue dress shirt and navy khaki trousers and black loafers.

I shake my head as Pam chokes out. "I…might need a soda or something like that…to settle my stomach Pop."

"Why does a tough Marine need to settle her stomach down?" Maria asks and she's still on the outs as far as Pam is concerned.

Pam shakes her head. "Why Ma; why are you continuing this fight? I'm trying to do my job, in spite of the fact I was shot yesterday; so why are we still dancing in the ring like two prize fighters?"

"Because we, your family, are trying to look out for you! You are in constant danger all the time!"

"Maria!" Gus yells as Maria stops. "Accept it; our daughter is a cop; danger is part of her job. Stop trying to changer her, protect her, or otherwise deter and shame her into being what she's chosen. It's time you made peace and stop acting like some damned war mare at Troy!"

I never heard Gus mention the historical war against Troy. And then I see Pam's attention perk up. This is a warning to me something's going on and so does Pam. Thea looks to Gus, "Problem Dad?"

"Oh nothing to worry about sweetheart…minor business stuff," Gus shrugs off his answer. Now I'm noticing the secretive ticks in Gus and Maria. Maybe I'm slipping as I get closer to the ripe old age of fifty. I could swear these personality ticks were not there two days ago.

And Gus seemed happy about where Pam lived and worked.

"Well Pop, if it's a money issue, Joe and I might be able to help." Pam offers as I nod. Gus grimaces; another odd facial tick that was not there before. "Pop?"

Gus shakes his head and then smiles. "Sorry honey; it's not a money issue. It's a personality issue inside Greek Town. We'll work it out."

Pam nods and then looks to Maria as she continues to frown. "Incidentally, Ma, I wanted the soda because I almost puked a half-hour ago. Three severed heads were delivered to the 18th District early this morning."

"Ew!" Romy squints.

"Cool!" Leo's eyes light up with excitement.

"I'm with you Romy," Thea and her family agree. I see Jason and Jennifer shake their heads at Pam's announcement. "Sis, you know these…severed heads?"

"Yes, I had dealings with all three of them. Problem is; I have an alibi for when these people were killed. So Ma can stop looking at me like I'm an alien or…xeno!" Maria jumps back at Pam's assertion and I shake my head. "Anyway, before we can close that case due to the dead, we need to confirm DNA and retinal scans."

"What need is there for DNA and retinal scans if your crooks are dead sis?" Thea asks as if she doesn't know the answer.

Pam smiles as she sounds off. "TFCC, the FBI Violent Crimes Task Force, the State Department and a few other interested parties, need confirmation before we close the cases of Alexi Krontzky, Tatyana Brezhnev, and the recently discovered Marine Major impostor Marko Kirov. DNA, with today's technology, can be faked. Retinal scans can't; which is why the two-step confirmation process."

"So now…you'll look into these dead Russians?" Gus's curiosity now concerns me. It sounds as if he fears someone will make a critical discovery.

However, Pam puts his fears to rest. "Nah, I'll let the FBI, or some Mob task-force handle it." Then Jason's cell phone rings. He answers and quietly discusses something else.

Jason hangs up and nods to Jennifer. "We need to go back to Naval Station Great Lakes. NCIS concluded the Murphy family investigation. Frank's been completely cleared of any wrongdoing."

"Good; one less thing for me to worry about." Pam smiles; then she asks, "Jen, any word on Kat or your parents?"

"No word; until Mom knows for a fact it's safe to come home…they won't. Even if the main families hunting Kat are eliminated, someone else might pick up the contract and then I'll be in the middle of it again." Jennifer looks to Gus and Maria. This sets Pam's bullshit detector off. "And if it's not the Russians who did this, and their actions resulted in the deaths of three of my detectives and patrol officers, I will return, and it won't be as a cop! I will do what I have to do to protect my family! I'm sure you can understand that…right Gus?"

"Absolutely Jen; no issues here," Gus smiles, but Pam and I still wonder what's going on here. "Anyway, I originally asked if anyone was hungry."

"The kids might be; I'm still wondering if I may get that soda please?" Pam asks as Gus nods. "Hey Marsha, would you get the kids a snack and me a soda? Put it on Pop's tab."

"Gustav!" Maria cries out.

Gus points his finger at her, "Not another word, or you'll be stuck at home dealing with Mrs. Corelli all day!"

Pam shakes her head as she hugs Jennifer and I shake Jason's hand. Jennifer whispers in Pam's ear. "Watch your six around your family. I think someone in this community is connected to your dead mobsters."

"Joe's got mine and I got his; safe travels to NS Great Lakes…and beyond!" Jennifer and Jason nod and leave as Pam sits back down and the waitress brings the soda and the snack for Romy and Leo.

"Well, as soon as Jen and Jace get back to Corpus, and Frank Murphy gets his family buried; I'll probably get recalled back to Texas too."

"What about us?" Romy asks as Leo nods.

"Oh, you think we forgot about you two? No way; you short Greek kids don't get off that easy. You're stuck like glue to us…isn't that right Mrs. Martinez?"

The Hispanic Social worker smiles as she hands Pam a folder. "We searched high and low to find a suitable family related to the kids and excluded the entire Williams clan in Arkansas. In fact, Little Rock informed the cult all the children will be placed with responsible foster families. With the blessings of the state of Illinois, Arkansas and Texas; I am happy to announce that you kids and you parents…have successfully adopted each other."

"What?" Pam asks as I do as the kids smile like imps. "What did you two do?"

Mrs. Martinez smiles at the group. "Romy and Leo enlisted the help of the Vaughns and had mutually binding adoption papers to sign; one set for you to adopt the kids and another set…for the kids to adopt you two. Everyone felt since you were still newlyweds, you needed to be adopted as well."

Unbelievable is my immediate thought as I dial Jason up. "Hey Squid; you and the pretty police chief…get your happy butts back here! Mrs. Martinez just ratted you two out!"

I hear the collective *damn* from both of them as Jason responds, *"We haven't even left the parking lot. We're coming back inside!"*

"Caught them just in time," I smile at Pam as she sighs. Then Jason and Jennifer walk back inside. As Pam and our little angels smile sadistically at our favorite couple from Texas, I ask, "You had parental adoption papers drawn up for Romy and Leo to sign for Pam and I? Have you two gone plumb loco?"

"Hold on Mr. Hampton," Jennifer answers me formally. I see Pam eyeball her suspiciously. "Let us review: you wanted to adopt these poor waifs the moment you met them.

"They began to trust you because you treated them like children who needed love, attention, and a safe environment. On the same note; you two are a novice married couple and never had any kids of your own save the ones you've ever baby sat in your lives…until Romy and Leo came along. Hence…Mrs. Martinez spoke with the kids at great length the night Pam was shot. And she asked them three times, what do you two think of Joe and Pam Hampton…as potential parents."

Mrs. Martinez smiles as she rings in, "And each time I asked that, they said to me, 'If it were possible, we would like to adopt them…because we need them, and we think…they need us too.' No matter how it was phrased; the same basic answer came from them."

"So…even though we've had shouting matches, a small amount of distrust between us; you…still want the two of us as parents?" Pam's tears flow as both Romy and Leo nod. Slowly Pam takes off her sling and takes the kids into her arms. "My shoulder still hurts, but I'd be proud to be your mom." Both kiss Pam on each cheek as I take my turn at signing the adoption papers.

"May the Vaughns serve as witnesses Mrs. Martinez?"

"I wouldn't dream of leaving them out of this process," Mrs. Martinez smiles impishly as the sour expressions of Jason and Jennifer shake their heads and sign the paperwork as well. "There, that wasn't so bad was it?"

"We should've left hours ago," Jason growls as Jennifer looks blankly at him.

Fifteen

"Oh my God Pam; the kids are adorable!" Mama Lucinda seems to find their appearance tolerable compared to the before photos we sent. *"My only question is…why are they bald?"*

"Grandma Lou; I'm hoping I said you're name right?" Romy smiles as Mom smiles back at her. "We…were rescued from human trafficking; and when Joe and Pam were asked to look after us. We were dirty, hadn't eaten in half-a-day, and had a bad case of head lice. Leo and I chose to be bald so we can grow a clean head of hair."

My dad smiles as he sees Romy as a potential granddaughter. *"And what are your full names again...Romy...right?"*

"I am Andromeda Christina Drivas...now Hampton. And Leo's full name is Leonidas Timothy Drivas...now Hampton. And we are very honored to be part of your family sir."

"Oh God, she called me sir *and not* Grandpa. *Joseph, what am I going to do with Romy; give her back to the Trojans?"*

Romy's wit quickens as her exposure to my father increases. "Seriously, you'd give me to the Trojans? Perhaps, Sir Geoffrey, upon our return to Corpus Christi, I should challenge you to a game of chess?"

Mom looks at Dad's profile and laughs, *"Respond to that…smart aleck! Based on that response, those kids will fit well in this family!"*

"I agree my dear and Romy...I'd be delighted to accept your chess challenge. When can we expect you four to get back?"

"Not an easy question to answer Geoff," Pam fidgets. "Those Russian families that chased Kat Petrov underground? All three of the capos here, ended up beheaded and their heads delivered to the 18th Police District."

Dad sits there silently. I never seen him just sit there; speechless on anything related to law enforcement. *"I've only heard of this sort of thing being done in Philadelphia.*

"And only when the Armenian or Russian Mobs try to take over Greek Mob interests or being a threat to Greek families of Mob associations."

"Hey Jace, Jen; would you mind playing aunt and uncle to the kids please? I think Joe and I will be up awhile. Hey guys, hugs and kisses good night; we'll see you in the morning." Romy and Leo come up and kiss us good night and go with Jason and Jennifer. Once out of earshot, Pam continues, "Who do you suspect of being Greek Mob in Chicago?"

"Too many; no one specific. I know that one Greek Mob faction in Chicago calls themselves Tau Omega. *Here's the problem: they never get involved in what is considered illegal businesses."*

"Wait; nothing at all?" Pam asks. Dad shook his head. "No drugs, numbers, arms, prostitution/human trafficking, or protection rackets? What do they do; operate legal operations and pay each other via favors and mutual protection?"

"That's what local intelligence in Chicago's telling us Pam," Mom answers as she pulls up a report and displays it split screen. I think Mom's getting computer lessons from Cody. *"Mostly five to ten merchants in Greek Town. And if other crime syndicates come within a frog's hair of entry; they have to pay a toll or get beheaded. Sounds pretty medieval if you ask me."*

"Sounds pretty medieval to me too," I say out loud as Pam and I gaze at one another. "Now I understand everything; the airport, the disowning, the constant bickering and then your father's odd behavior today…"

"Babe; you're not thinking…?"

"I don't want to think what I'm thinking. But look at it from this angle for a moment; out of all the family members on either side, daughters are always special. Why; because when married to the right man, they bring forth life…new generations being born." Wow, I put it together; but why would Gus go to all this trouble? Then it hits me like a lightning bolt; this all started the day Pam married Charlie Dupree.

"Now I understand why Gus was so…vengeful sounding when the Dupree came calling in Dallas, and later in Corpus Christi; Charlie's knowledge would have exposed his operation."

Pam sits back in tears. All her life, Gus told her to work hard, appreciate her opportunities and love her family fiercely. Now, all the suppositions and all the maneuvering, wasn't to protect her family; it was to draw the Russians into a trap…to be killed. And Gus or whomever in her family used her and the cops as bait. "Joe, your folks and the kids are my family; my only family now."

"Your father might not be involved." I say that, but I can't honestly stop thinking it's not true. All the references of why Pam was the family explorer; how she escaped all the corruption and the sense of alienation. Now I understand why Gus spoke in those terms. And now, Pam knows why too. "Okay, we're both thinking this and neither wants to admit it. What's next?"

"We take the kids and go home with Jason, Jennifer, TFCC, Quid, and Murph. I got a call from him saying he cremated all the bodies including his father's. I'll tell Thea we're leaving, but no one else. I don't know who to and who not to trust here anymore." Then she looks to the two wonderful people on the laptop screen. "Geoff, Lou; we'll be home probably tomorrow, and we'll be towing back those sweet, bald-headed children."

"Well, this old copper has one thing to say, I'm glad we have grandchildren involved now. I believe the responsibility will galvanize your marriage in a way you never thought possible." Although Dad's being subtle; I can tell he's jumping up and down inside like an energetic five-year old. He and Mom wait for years until I finally marry and now, they're grandparents.

And I smile as well as laugh, "Well copper, let me put this new family into perspective for you."

My father appropriately gasps. You think he's waited to play this part like a Shakespearian actor? *"Egads...perspective; from my issue? How will the world interpret that?"*

"Very carefully I'm sure Geoff," Pam smiles, "And I'll assist with the perspective angle. The kids had papers drawn up…to adopt us!"

"*What?*" Mom asks with shock in her voice. "*Those sweet little urchins adopted you two? And did the state of Illinois actually kept a copy of this paperwork?*"

"Scary…huh Lou? We've signed for them; they signed for us. We're stuck with each other now!"

"*And based on what you've told us about the kids; that's a good thing. Pam, did you tell your folks what the OB-GYN's told you?*"

"I did; they didn't take it well. And Mom almost tried to annul my marriage to Joe and marry me off to some Greek family I never met before. I didn't know how scared she really was about me being a cop until now." Pam tries to think and…articulate the situation. "I think she was more scared of me…finding all this out."

"*Or…what you might try to do to stop it.*" Mom makes an excellent point.

"Lou, I gotta know…if you knew…?"

Mom sighs and she understands why Pam has to ask. "*No, and I didn't know for sure…until you confirmed some theories. Pam, I knew your mother's fears were totally irrational, but I also felt like she did at times when Joe was a Marine and NCIS. And that's partly why I might have enabled her concerning you. Now that I know what Dupree did to you, I'm not about enabling anymore.*"

"Thanks Lou; you and Geoff mean the world to me. I hope Joe and I do half as well as you two did with Joe and John."

"*Pam, you may have many imperfections, but all human beings do. But from what we can see here, you have become a positive influence on Romy and Leo…they love you two. And that's not going to change. Your parents, regardless of yours or our suspicions…love you as well. But in this case, everyone has a choice to make. Just…try not to burn any bridges you can't rebuild.*" Dad has great advice at times; but I'm not sure if Pam's going to heed it this round.

"Easier said than done; I'm going to bed. Love you guys," Pam blows kisses to my folks as she kisses me on the cheek; then heads to bed.

"*Joe?*" Mom's gentle voice rings in my ears. "*She's balancing on the edge of a dagger; be careful and watch your six son.*"

"Always Mom. We love you guys…good night." Now, what do we do if Gus and Maria are involved in Tau Omega? As I head to bed with a household minus the Vaughns, I walk up behind Pam and hug her. "I just checked on the kids and let Jason and Jennifer out to go back to NS Great Lakes." Pam nods as she gently grabs my arms with her right hand and puts her left around my waist. "You know we'll get through this right? Tau Omega may not even be involved with the dead Russians."

"Maybe, then again…maybe not; but I do know once we find out for sure, protecting Romy and Leo becomes our first priority…as family."

Sixteen

This morning we meet with Thea and her family for breakfast at NS Great Lakes and with Asst. Dir. Vale's permission, we give them a tour of the NCIS Field Office. "This is the squad room; some call it a Rogue's gallery, and some call it a bullpen, like in baseball."

"Did you ever work for…N-C-I-S; Aunt Pam?" Sean asks as he looks up at the ceiling.

Pam smiles as does Thea and Mike. "No, I was more like that Marine over by the door. Excuse me Gunny, would you come over here a second please?" The gunny nods to the Marine next to her and meets us. "Good morning Gunnery Sgt. Baker, I am Captain Pamela Papadakis Hampton; I am the Major Case Commander for Corpus Christi's Police Department. I used to be a Marine Corps MP command officer and I was wondering; would you please brief my nephews Liam and Sean how MPs and Shore cops in the Navy, coordinate law enforcement with NCIS?"

The brown-haired gunny with the tight bun and hazel eyes nods to us. "Be glad to ma'am. So, your names are Liam and Sean? I am GSG Alison Baker, but you guys can call me Aly. Shall we ask your dad to come along? I hear he used to be a JAG lawyer…in the Army…yuck!" The kids laugh at GSG Baker's joke and even Mike appreciates it. I nod at Romy and Leo so they could tag along.

Thea gives Pam the suspicious eye as we walk upstairs toward MTAC. "You remember Joe telling you about MTAC?" Thea nods. "Well, NCIS Asst. Dir. Leo Vale's given us permission to look it over, but no video or audio please?"

"No problem," Thea smiles as we enter MTAC. As we enter, an operation is in progress. "Where's that at Joe?"

"Lightning, is that Dallas or Corpus Christi?" I ask NCIS SSA Lightning McCoy who punches a few keys at his monitoring station.

After a few moments, I recognize the CCPD building on John Sartain Street from downtown. "Take a look ladies."

Pam and Thea walk up as one of their cousins, James Constantine, is being escorted inside the building in handcuffs. Pam shakes her head as Thea looks up and extends her right hand. "What the hell Pam? Did you know about this...arrest?"

"No, I didn't; but I did know that Jennifer had her suspicions of our father...being a *Godfather of the Night?* One thing about Chief Vaughn is when she's bored, Google becomes her best friend. She did lots and lots of research on the Greek Mafia; goes all the way back to Athens in the Old Country. My question, without violating attorney-client privilege; how do they relate to the Papa Papadakis Restaurant chain?"

Thea finds the closest seat and sits down with tears in her eyes. "It all makes sense now."

"What, Thea, what makes sense?" I ask as if I couldn't guess.

"For the last...four years, Dad brought me incorporation paperwork to invest in several businesses in Greek Town. Mom and Pop shops mostly; nothing of significant value." Thea looks up with tears in her eyes and just sobs. "Why did he do this Pam?"

I'm not at a loss on this. The timeline of Gus's business insulation; coincides with Pam's exile from New Orleans to Dallas. And the timing also indicates Gus hoped Pam would return to Chicago, but she stayed in Dallas, met, and married me in Corpus Christi earlier this year. In his and Maria's minds, it all went south. Finally, Pam offers a thought. "Because we are special to him...Thea; because daughters are special to fathers. He went...to all this trouble...to protect those most precious to him. What he didn't expect, was the local Russian mob to be hunting the sister of the CCPD Police Chief; and that made all the difference since she was my Chief Hostess."

"Jen's pain became his...because of her friendship with you," Thea shakes her head in disbelief. "That's why they wanted you to stop interfering with the Murphy case.

"Angelo was in on it too! Then it was out of their hands when NCIS assumed jurisdiction. I can see why Ma kept trying to get in the middle of it now."

"No," Pam squints, "Ma just won the Oscar for Best Actress in a Greek Comedic Tragedy! They played us, every time we were there."

Thea adds, "To delay you, every step in your investigation; they committed obstruction at every turn. And then prevented you from hunting Krontzky and his cronies by doting on Romy and Leo. Remind me after you leave, to go and kill our parents please?"

"Nope; no can do sis," Pam smiles as she stands Thea up and hugs her. "You, as an officer of the court, know better than to ask me that." Pam squishes Thea's cheeks to where her lips pucker. "Trust your baby sister on this one."

"You're squishing my cheeks together!" Thea mumbles as Pam let's go. Then Jason and Jennifer enter. Jason's decked out in denim trousers, red polo golf shirt and brown boots while Jennifer stuns in a blue denim dress with brown sandals. "Well, you two look like you're ready to travel."

"Yes, I've missed the Gulf and my daughter. Jason and I are ready to get back home. Thea, I've enjoyed getting to know you and your immediate family again. Your boys are precious." And Jennifer means every word as she embraces Thea.

"Thank you, for coming here and backing my sister up; even when she felt her entire family abandoned her you and TFCC never did. I'm…grateful beyond words." Then Thea asks curiously, "What will happen to our cousin, James Constantine?"

Jennifer shakes her head as Jason comments. "I discovered he left Chicago late two nights ago; after the heads were delivered to the 18th District. Federal Air Marshals caught him flying out of O'Hare and landing at Corpus Christi International early yesterday afternoon. TSO officials at the airport found a blood-covered machete in his possession. And he had a letter in his possession.

"The translation reads, 'Eliminate the Russian bitch and...anyone related to her.' With Jen and I here, how am I supposed to interpret that Thea?"

Thea sobs again as Pam and I shake our heads in disbelief. We are left speechless at the potential...horror Tau Omega plans to unleash on the Vaughn family. Jennifer speaks to Jason's question. "I do know five Russians related to the Krontzky, Brezhnev and Kirov families were shot and killed just as they trespassed on the Flying V Ranch in Snyder. And not too far behind, two Greeks from Athens were arrested for carrying illegal firearms. Our family is safe. You might tell your father to lay off of my sister Kat Petrov. I can't be held responsible on how...protective my mother is at this point."

"And I don't blame her," all eyes focus on Pam after her comment. "You remember when I told you not to do anything?" Thea nods. "Others will handle this problem from here on out. And you can make a clean break."

"How?" Thea asks the one-word question.

"Move your family to Texas; you said you have a law credential in all fifty states, right? Each major city needs attorneys with all kinds of credentials Thea." Pam's answer instills an inner conflict within Thea. Her loyalty to her family versus the love of the family she brought into the world; are powerful forces she must combat. Pam bows her head; then takes Thea's hands into hers. "All I'll say is this: I love you and your family. I left Chicago because I couldn't deal with all its history, its violence, its death; and went to live with Aunt Ruth. Then I learned why there is a history of violence, of death when I became a Marine; then a cop. And after one failed marriage to an evil, sadistic bastard, I met Joe and my life is now complete."

Thea smiles, "Just like I met Mike and my life became complete. We met two guys outside of our cultural norms and our parents have difficulty with our choices. It's like we broke some unwritten rule about dating non-Greeks; then marrying them.

"What is their problem?"

"You chose to buck tradition; and so you gave thousands of years of Greek tradition a kick in the pants," Jennifer smiles. "Thea, Pam; you are both wives and mothers now. Your parents desired those titles for you but didn't know how you'd achieve them. But how you've achieved them disappoints them. They fear you won't remember who you are and your origins. I believe you will; like I remembered mine."

Jason sighs, "Let's return to the squad room. I think Mike and the kids are back."

Before we start downstairs, Jennifer spies three familiar people: a chestnut-haired woman with greenish blue eyes and full smile with dimples and a fashionable outfit; her father, head clean-shaven with a beak nose and toothless grin. His own ensemble stylish for a man of his years. A younger version in a beautiful sundress and sandals. But around the necks of each is a necklace with a beeping light. Pam and the rest notice the small indentions on each necklace as small blocks of Semtex. "Pamela!" Pam looks down as her Uncle Sal holds up a detonator. "Your father requires a meeting with you and your sister. Come quietly and no one gets hurt."

Pam turns to Jennifer and shakes her head. "I didn't think...my father capable of this Jen. I'm sorry!" Pam scowls at Sal as she descends the stairs. She looks up to me, smiles and nods. I nod to GSG Baker who tosses me her M-16 assault weapon. I look down as Sal looks up at me and I point it at him. "I'm not negotiating with you Sgt. Salvatore Constantine. And I will not go see my father. Instead, you're going to play this by my rules. Anyone gets hurt; I kill you for committing a terrorist act on a federal reservation!"

Seventeen

What is Joseph doing?" Sal asks nervously as he glares up into my eyes. He knows I'm an old sniper and not afraid of threading a needle as Jason and I used to call it. Pam walks up and draws her Glock and points it flush against Sal's forehead. "Have you lost your mind?" Then I see Pam cock the hammer back. Sal starts to sweat.

Pam's cool as a cucumber as Lightning deploys a signal jammer to disable the detonator. "Pam, the detonator's useless! The signal's jammed!"

"Thank you Lightning! It's time I found out which of us has true faros; me, or Sal!" Pam continues to hold the muzzle of her Glock against Sal's forehead. "You have a choice: shit or get off the toilet!" Sal hands the detonator to one of Vale's NCIS agents and Scott Lassiter walks up and cuff's Sal's hands behind his back. "Salvatore Constantine, you are under federal arrest for the commission of an act of terror on a US federal reservation. You will have: no Miranda, no right to an attorney. In simple language you old bastard; you're an enemy combatant of the United States of America and subject to incarceration at one of our prisons holding enemy combatants. He's all yours Agent Lassiter."

I come down from the fourth floor with Jennifer hugging Katerina her sister all the way down. GSG Baker retrieves her weapon from me and I sit down, drained by the excitement. Vale walks over to me. "Joe, you okay?"

"I'm getting tired of all this adrenaline rush. It's about to give me heart failure!" Everyone roars with laughter as Romy and Leo run up and hug me. "Oh I'm so glad you two are here to help me calm down!"

"We were worried about you and Mom...Dad!" Leo utters the sweet music of my new title...Dad. "I never saw anyone handle guns like you two."

"Well you and your sister lucked out; you have Marines for parents…and that's not a bad thing." I say that as Jason nods in agreement.

Jennifer walks over and embraces, this is a surreal thought: my children. "You know; your mom needs hugs too. In fact, she's crying and probably could use some hugs and kisses from you guys."

I watch as my children go over and hug as well as kiss their mom. Pam's tears dry a little as the kids shower her with hugs and kisses. Mike, Thea and the Morans walk over to where I sit and marvel with me the interactions of my family. Grace bends down next to me as I ask, "How does it feel to be back home?"

"Much better than on the run Joe," Grace smiles as she watches my children and my wife. "Jen told me what you did for them; and how they had Child Services draw up papers to adopt you and Pam! I thought that was hilarious!"

"Hilarious…yes; was it logical, it's anyone's guess. But Grace, I wouldn't trade them for anything or anyone." And I'm being truthful; Pam and I love these crazy kids. And you have to respect the fact they adopted us as well. "Pam and I feel blessed beyond reason right now."

Pam and our children walk up to us. "Joe's right Grace, we do feel blessed beyond reason. I have a loving husband, loving children, friends who love me. And a sister and her family who love and accept me as is; flaws and all. This is my family."

"And a wonderful family it is sis," Thea's remark gets a hug from my children. However, Thea steps back and observes the rest of the family members who accompanied Sal to NCIS. She bumps her shoulder against Pam. "What about them?"

"Oh yes, thank you for reminding me Thea." She turns to face all the family-related cops in the room. "Ladies and gentlemen of the Papadakis, Constantine, Aniston, and Kapelos families; you accompanied a police sergeant who just attempted, what can loosely be interpreted as a terrorist act, to a federal reservation.

"Do I have to spell out how much trouble each and every one of you is in at this moment?" Everyone shakes their heads as to the potential charge each one faces. "Good; now I'm going to make this simple: all who know the identity of the *Godfather of the Night*, but choose to obstruct the case at this point, go over to Agent Lassiter's desk. "You will remove your law enforcement creds, your weapon and place them in the evidence bags provided."

Under Sheriff Adam Kapelos smiles, "And what if we resist?"

Vale roars, "Then I and my agents will kill you dead! You...feelin' frisky?"

As Vale stands in Adam Kapelos' face, the broad-shouldered Under Sheriff backs down. "No, not that frisky."

"Good," Pam says with a condescending tack in her voice. "Now, as I said before I was rudely interrupted, if you plan on being a pain in my ass, go over and turn in your side arms and creds to Agent Lassiter. The consequence: if you make me take everyone's creds and guns away, and I find out you backed Sal, your life will have ten times the hell he'll experience!"

Vale yells, "Move your asses now!" Every member of the Constantine and Kapelos families all march over and form a line at Scotty's desk. Boop and Manny go over and assist in getting all the evidence bags processed. When Pam moves over by Vale, he whispers, "You've done outstanding work Pam."

"It doesn't feel that outstanding Leo. It sorts of feels like...when SEAL Team Five left Jason behind in Desert Storm. Someone in my family, wanted me to be someone I'd never be; and now everyone's suffering for that decision."

Then Leo Vale sees I'm only thinking. "By separating the families like this; you know who will speak to us and keep them protected. And here I thought Marines weren't that bright as far as battle strategy."

Pam shakes her head. "Funny squid; you should know by now Marines are like SEALs; we can survive on land and air just like them in the sea."

Vale laughs, "And I also forget female Marines are smarter!" Both laugh as I continue to watch the Constantine and Kapelos families drop their creds and side arms. After each one's stuff gets dropped, all turn and glare at Pam like she's a perp. And she blew kisses at each one. "You still have a large group in your family and the Aniston bunch. If you need to take a break, we can manage. Besides, you have kids to nurture now...Mom!" Just as Vale says that, our children rush up and bear hug Pam. "And there's my proof; you are loved a great deal."

"I've been telling Pam that the last three years!" Okay, it's time I join the family love fest and assert my hug rights. Romy breaks off and latches on to me. "See, Uncle Leo, even I'm loved!"

"Well, I have to take into account the poor girl's only known you for a day-and-a-half working on three." Vale's jibe at my personality receives all the groans and cat calls from the whole squad room.

Romy light-heartedly chuckles at Vale's joke, "And Uncle Leo's a good friend of yours?"

"This is why your mother and I are fond of saying, 'With friends like these, who needs enemies?' Uncle Leo's a prime example!" My humor tends to bite ever so often, but Leo Vale knows I'm teasing. What gets me is my *son* Leo coming over to meet his *Uncle* Leo; talk about confusing. "My dear son Leonidas; this is your adoptive Uncle from SEAL Team Three Leonardo Vale."

"Pleased to meet you...Nephew Leo."

I'm pleased to meet you too...Uncle Leo!" Both shake hands as they turn to Pam and I; and flash wicked grins at us.

"Oh I can sense the trouble now," Jason walks up and leans on Uncle Leo. "Are you trying to be a bad influence on this young man?"

Vale looks back at Jason and slowly shakes his head; as he turns to face Leo. "You see, Leo, what I put up with on a daily basis?"

"Oh don't start that, 'what I put up with' nonsense. If I were to bring your family in here and question them, what would they say about you?"

I ask so Jason's spared any future ribs of Leo Vale's antics.

"You see Leo, I lose all credibility when I'm around your dad and Uncle Jason," Vale smiles as little Leo laughs with him. Vale looks over at Pam and asks me, "You think she'll be okay Joe?"

I nod. "She'll weather this storm Leo. I can't say the same for her family structure, but she'll come through it okay."

And as I continue to watch Pam, she walks up to Rudy and his girls. Pam's Aunt, Regina Aniston, joins them. Her light brown, curly hair, and round face; denote her Greek heritage as dark navy pant suit compliments her white blouse and matching pumps. "Pamela, I never thought Sal would do something like this. And I can only suspect your father, my brother, of being involved."

"No proof at all…Thea Gina?" I see the lost look in Pam's eyes; hoping her Aunt Regina can give her answers and a 'why' all this happened.

Rudy offers some explanation Pam is able to stomach in the short term. "Business moves, financial favors, city councilman bribed; nothing solid anyone can tie to Gus at all. But we do know this; even crime families located all over Chicago, fear the Godfather of the Night, who runs Greek Town." Pam nods as Rudy asks his next question, "I'm guessing going to see your Pop is out of the question?"

"Would you trust him, if he held relatives of your best friend, hostage with explosives around their necks? Regardless who pushed the button?" Pam looks into Rudy's brown eyes for an answer.

Rudy's answer surprises even the Constantine contingent still being processed. "Pam, he's my brother and I love him. As far as trust goes," I see Rudy shake his head, "Not as far as I can throw him; and he knows it. I don't blame you for not wanting to go see him."

"Okay, in my line of sight; I have two of the wisest family members within law enforcement. And I am trying to rely on eight years of experience in the military, and twelve years as a civilian cop.

"Now here I am, thinking...that my father is an organized crime figure. For the first time in my life as a cop; I don't...know what to do." Pam fights back the bitter tears that refuse to dry. "What do I do?"

Rudy takes my sobbing wife into his arms as Ariel and Nikki join the embrace. "Sometimes, not doing anything...is doing something. You can make yourself crazy with the 'what if's' all day long. At the end of the day, you still need hard evidence to nail anyone involved in organized crime."

But I see 'Thea' Gina, as she likes all the kids to call her, walk up with a gentle hand on my wife's shoulder. "Captain of your own unit in CCPD, married to a gorgeous former Marine like yourself, adopting kids, and serving up potential terrorists on a federal reservation. Not bad for a day-and-a-half's work as an Acting Asst. Chief Super." Pam laughs as does the rest. "Did you know, your name means 'All honey' in Greek? Your father named you that because he said you were the sweetest baby he ever held. I think he still feels that way."

"Then why is he making this so difficult...Thea Gina?"

Regina smiles like Pam does when she's feeling impish, like now. "Your father...wants Rudy and me, to talk you out of whatever it is he thinks you're going to do. Here's the problem Rudy and I face; you're too damned good at your job to fall for our sloppy advice!" Everyone laughs again. Then Regina continues, "So, I can offer good advice here. Because I work for CPD's Organized Crime Bureau too, I sometimes get to play in the same sandbox as the FBI's Organized Crime Bureau. Like the Mob, we do favors for one another. When your father started incorporating the restaurant chain, and not including the rest of the family in on the business decisions, the FBI came to me asking questions. I told them get the authorizations you need and get to work."

"What did they tell you recently?" Pam has to ask. The suspense alone is killing her.

Regina sighs, "He's into some pretty shady stuff kiddo. Wiretaps are focusing in on the deaths of the three Russian capos here in Chi-town."

"Anything conclusive?"

"Nothing yet; but your dad has the discipline of a Marine; no offense Rudy?"

"None taken sis," Rudy smiles.

"While we're on the subject; confiscate the phones of those officers and deputies please?" Pam yells.

Lightning McCoy, his wife Leah, Manny and Boop Garcia; all go around collecting cell phones. I see Lightning struggle with Sal as he pushes hard on his phone. Lightning sees the text sent as Sal laughs maniacally. "You're too late; I've warned Gus!"

"And by now, the FBI has all the warrants it needs to go in and shut all of Gus's restaurants down," Regina smiles as Sal's smile falls to the ground. Regina walks over with a swagger Pam hasn't seen in ages. "What did my brother want with his daughters Salvatore?"

"Lawyer," Sal smiles and then announces, "And Athena or Mike will serve in that capacity."

To everyone's surprise, except for mine and Pam's, Mike and Thea laugh like clowns at a clown convention. Thea stops and looks at the look of surprise on Sal's face. "Wait, hold on one second; you want me to be your attorney of record? Okay, here's my advice: confess your sins to the feds, name names within the Greek Mob in Chicago, and tell how you planned on murdering three people if my sister and I refused to play along with my father! And then, cut the best deal for yourself because anything short of that; is a big hell no from my husband and I!"

Sal mumbles, "Disloyal...little...bitches!"

Pam turns and I see a glare in her eyes I've only seen for Angelo or some perp. The scary part; Thea has the same glare in her eyes too. Mike walks up beside me. "Are they about to do what I think they're about to do?"

"I believe so Mike. Jace, Jen; would you take all the kids into the upstairs conference room please? The next few moments, aren't for their little eyes to see?" And as Jason and Jennifer escort the kids upstairs and disappear, Pam and Thea give Sal a thug beat-down only two angry sisters can dish out. With each punch or kick; you could hear Sal grunt and cry out in pain. After a minute or two, Pam and Thea sit a bleeding and bruised Uncle Sal in the closest chair.

"Now, any of you other Constantine or Kapelos family members want a solid ass-kicking?" Pam yells. Everyone else shook their heads!

Eighteen

Saturday morning rolls around as Pam, Romy, Leo, and I pack up and prepare to return to Corpus Christi. To our surprise as we start to load up, Pam's sister Thea, her husband Mike, and Liam as well as Sean; all roll up with Uncle Rudy and Ariel and Nikki as escorts. "Well, we're getting a royal send-off here. What's all this guys?" Pam asks as Thea's smile radiates our little VIP bungalow at NS Great Lakes. "What?"

Thea lowers her eyes a little, "With everything that's happened the last day or two; Mike and I talked it over last night. We think you're right–starting over in Texas isn't such a bad idea. In fact, Jennifer called and said she found us a house not too far from her. How is she as a neighbor?"

Of course I have to smile at this question. I don't have the heart to tell Thea, Jen probably had the realtor reserve the house between us for Mike, Thea, and their boys. As if I could keep it a secret, Pam spills the beans. "She's not too bad; being the fact she's the police chief and my boss." Thea's eyes widen as Pam smiles. "The Vaughns live two houses down from us. And, the house in between theirs and ours has been reserved for you."

Thea starts to cry as she throws her arms around Pam. "How do I thank you for your generosity?"

"It's not generosity; you're family and I love doing nice things for my family," Pam smiles as she hugs Thea again. "We need to get moving. We have to drive over to Midway International to catch our flight."

"Why Midway; why not O'Hare?" Mike asks innocently.

"Jason's family has an international business foundation and one of their perks is a fleet of Lear jets that are moored at all Signature Flight terminals across the globe. So, you get to travel in style," I say as Thea's eyes light up with excitement.

When we arrive, Jason and Jennifer are standing by and waiting for us. "I thought you guys were on your way to Corpus," I cry as I see Gus and Maria inside the terminal. "What the hell are they doing here?"

Jennifer stretches her neck so she can articulate her outrage. "Your father has a goon squad surrounding the jet. If we try to board, he threatened to kill us. So, he wants five minutes of your time as well as Thea's; then we can leave." Pam smooths her hair back as she bobs her head up and down. "Tell me you have a backup plan Pam?"

"Let's go talk to my father; and roll the FBI's Violent Crime Task Force," Pam smiles as does Jennifer. We all walk up to the plane as Gus's soldiers point P-90 Assault weapons at everyone. "My, my; you're going to kill everyone if we fail to comply with your wishes...Godfather of the Night?" At that signal, the task force Rudy works fly up to the terminal, as well as CPD's OCB.

Rudy dives behind a bullet-proof door and yells, "Drop them or get dropped!" When Gus's soldiers move, all the adults heading back to Corpus Christi, draw a side arm and kill six of the ten soldiers, Gus ordered to surround the jet. "Again, for those who remain, drop them or get dropped!"

"Drop them boys; no need for anyone else to die here today," Gus yells as he glares at Pam and Thea. The Vaughns, Mike and I; don't even rate acknowledgement at this point. "Did you have to kill six of my men?"

"Did you have to commit a federal crime by illegally detaining a jet bound all points south?" Pam shakes her head and looks at her father like he's crazy. "You do realize you committed a federal crime for this alleged five minute conversation?" Gus sighs as Pam increases the pressure; he really didn't think this through I imagine. "You wasted two-and-a-half minutes of time due to this little stunt; talk fast!"

"Someone killed the Russians as a message to the other families; don't mess with my family.

"And because I can...influence many people in Chicago due to my ties to the community, no one will dare challenge me. I would think a police captain from Corpus Christi, would appreciate some of the pressure removed due to being shot here."

"Except one little point of order; Mr. Papadakis," Pam points out and now she's getting formal, which means Gus is about to get a verbal ass-kicking. "What about the three collar bombs around Gerald and Grace Moran, as well as Grace's daughter Katerina? How do you explain that away Mr. Papadakis?"

"I don't like it when you talk like that..."

"How is that a problem? Is it because I sound like a cop and not your daughter? Or is it because when Sal appeared with those bombs around hostage's necks, he thought I'd fold like cops in all those hostage movies and scenarios he read about in old reports?" Pam stops and lets that all hang for a moment; then continues. "Instead, I challenged him with a sniper pointing an M-16 at his head, while holding a Glock nine millimeter to his forehead. He learned very quickly, after I announced he violated the Patriot Act, he was done! Every member of his family present, as well as members of the Kapelos family present, are all going to GITMO; branded as enemy combatants of the United States of America. So, I will ask this question; which of you ordered him to throw his life away, for the sake of the family: you or Ma?"

When Gus gives Maria the evil eye and Maria lowers her eyes, Pam knows who sent Sal to NS Great Lakes with the Semtex necklaces. "Why, why did you do this Maria?"

Maria lightly shakes her head. "They...were a threat. Jennifer's family, her sister, all the cops connected to both cases, even Mike and Joe; they are a threat to this family! If our daughters had married Greek sons; none of this misery would exist!" Maria points her finger in Gus's face. "I blame you and our daughters for this misery!"

Pam slowly steps up to Maria and smiles like a cobra.

"Well, since we caused all this misery for you, Mrs. Papadakis, I have nothing else to say to you." Before Pam turns completely to board the jet, she turns on her heel and issues a warning. "If you just so much as screw up a frog's hair in this situation, I will return with an army and reign hell fire down on your pointed head! Do you get my message, Mrs. Papadakis?"

Maria's eyes well up with tears. For a second time in three days, Pam essentially told her she was dead to Pam. She nods, but the shock she experiences that accents the moment, comes from her eldest daughter Thea. After they embrace and kiss, Thea drops her bombshell. "Pam's short-sighted. She should have hugged and kissed you prior to making her threat...Mrs. Papadakis."

Both Gus and Maria display horror-filled expressions as Thea continues, "Did you know, in addition to the Russians killing three of Pam's officers, James Constantine was arrested with hand-written orders to locate and kill Jennifer Vaughn, her entire family, and any one left connected to that case? Did you even consider, he'd also kill Pam, not to mention me, the moment this came here to Chicago?"

Maria shakes her head as her tears fall. Gus yells, "Stop this Thea!"

"Yes, I will stop this Mr. Papadakis; and I'll stop with this: you have no daughters left. You are dead to me, my sister, and our families!" Both Gus and Maria crumble to the inner tarmac as Thea bends down and whispers, "Damn you both!" She rises and ushers her kids and family up into the jet.

Pam and I hang back as Jason and Jennifer usher Romy and Leo into the jet; then Jason and Jennifer return. Jennifer bends down and glares into Gus and Maria's eyes. "I will request the Asst. Dist. Attn. or the A-USA to offer no deal to James Constantine. And if I can connect him to what Pam's already done; he'll have a reunion with family members at GITMO." What Pam and I see next scares the bejesus out of us, as a Comanche war-shaman appears in Jennifer's face. The face of a mother wolf; protecting her pack.

"Come to Texas, Georgia or anywhere near the south, this face appears to you again...and you die; clear?"

"C-Crystal...C-Chief Vaughn," Gus ekes out as Jennifer rises and her face returns to normal. She boards the jet as we follow. Thirty minutes later, the jet takes flight; headed to Texas.

Two hours later, we land at Corpus Christi International at the Signature Flight terminal. I step off first as Romy, Leo, Liam, Sean, Mike, and Thea disembark, "Welcome to Corpus Christi, Texas!"

Liam observes we're still not outside yet. "Hey, wait a minute Uncle Joe; why did we pull in here?"

"We're waiting for our ride." I know; it's a cheesy answer to give to an eleven year old, but I'm the uncle; hence I give out cheesy answers. "Actually, the ride we're waiting on has a full welcome/security contingent." As if on cue, four black SUVs pull up and park. Out pops my brother John and out of the second vehicle pops Lt. Col. Brad Jessup of the Provost Marshal's office.

Jason walks up with me as John and Brad huddle with us. "What's going on fellas?" Jason asks as if someone just declared World War III.

"Several supporters of the Greek neighborhoods in Corpus Christi, want James Constantine released regardless of his crimes or alleged crimes," John shakes his head and looks to Pam and sighs.

"I'm guessing our departure from Chicago was less than a clean getaway?" Thea asks as John nods to her. "No surprise there; how do we handle this hiccup Jen?"

Jennifer smiles, "We hold a press conference."

Members of the Corpus Christi press gather at CCPD Headquarters on John Sartain Street. Inside the conference room where Jennifer and her staff hold weekly press briefings, several members of the press and the local Greek community, wait for a statement from Jennifer or Pam. Jennifer steps up to the mic.

"Good afternoon ladies and gentlemen. At five-thirty yesterday afternoon Central Standard Time, CCPD in conjunction with Task Force Corpus Christi, arrested Detective Grade One James Constantine of the Chicago Police Department. Upon his arrest, evidence confiscated from Det. Constantine lists as follows: one kilo of Semtex plastic explosive, one P-90 Assault Rifle, one Glock 17 nine millimeter pistol, and ten burner cell phones as possible detonators for IEDs in Corpus Christi. Also confiscated, was a bloody machete."

John Reynolds is a reporter I like. He did a feature piece on my firm and took a tour of our downtown offices. His motif matches that of the late Alfred Hitchcock, but with more dignity for an old country boy from Texas. "Chief Vaughn; with all this evidence accumulated against Det. Constantine, why is the local community requesting his arrest be vacated?"

"For the answer to that and other questions, I'm turning this press conference over to my Major Case Commander, Captain Pamela...Hampton."

Jennifer motions Pam to take the podium and center stage. "John, you know me due to some of the cases I've worked in recent months, how I will not give you political answers to your questions." John smiles and nods. "I will say this to appease the local Greek community. I will no longer associate myself with the family of Gustav Papadakis of Chicago, his wife Maria Constantine Papadakis, or even the Kapelos family of Chicago. Both the Constantine and Kapelos families grieved me by attempting to commit an act of terror at NS Great Lakes yesterday afternoon. Around the necks of Gerald and Grace Moran of Savannah, GA, and of recently immigrated Katerina Svetlana Petrov, were three Semtex bomb necklaces. Sgt. Salvatore Constantine held a detonator to kill these three people and anyone else; unless my sister and I met with my father Gustav.

"A tech with Task Force Corpus Christi present at the time activated a universal signal jammer to disable the detonator.

"Once the detonator was disabled, Sgt. Constantine and his confederates were arrested for violating the Patriot Act. This arrest resulted in the subsequent arrest of Det. Constantine here in Corpus Christi; as well as two unidentified Greek patrol officers from Chicago in Snyder, Texas.

"If you will all note on page three of the press release made available an hour ago, you will find these officers will also be declared enemy combatants of the United States of America." Then Gia Christakis of Channel 8 News holds up her hand. "Yes Gia?"

Gia Christakis is new to me as a reporter for Channel 8. Her dark hair, green eyes, and hour-glass shape, compliments her tailored tan business suit as she speaks into her mic. "Captain Hampton, what do you see as the long range...consequences for such a declaration made in Chicago?"

Pam takes time before she answers. However, Thea walks up and whispers and then nods. "Okay, ladies and gentlemen; this is my paternal sister, Athena Flynn. She is an attorney and has graciously volunteered to field that question. Thea?"

Thea steps up to the mic. "As you just heard, my sister calls me the short name...Thea. Now, Ms. Christakis, correct?" Gia smiles and nods. "As any Greek present here knows, the term 'Thea' actually means 'aunt' in the Greek language. So, I tell all my nieces and nephews to call me 'Aunt' Thea so I can use it as my nickname. But as to any long range consequences, we only see possible legal documents filed to declare us clan-less as far as having no family ties to our former family. The long range benefit is it will save Pam and I tons of legal headaches should those old family ties come under federal investigation. What we only suspect; can't hurt us." Thea looks to Jennifer, who smiles and nods. Then Pam whispers something and Thea returns to the press conference.

"It seems the cops have left me with you guys." The press corps chuckle all over the place as Thea leans up on the podium and smiles. "A bit of an announcement I was asked to relay to all of you.

"Captain Hampton is now a new mom to two wonderful kids who were caught up in the wildest human trafficking transaction in the history of law enforcement. It seems that their parents...were killed and the father's entire family line, to be illegally adopted by the mother's parents. And these nut jobs were part of some crazy cult in Arkansas. Now, as to their...lack of hair, I'll let Captain Hampton explain that."

"Gee thanks sis!" The press roars with laughter this time as my wife explains my children's lack of follicles. "So that I can properly articulate how this happened, would my family join me up here please?" Romy, Leo, and I walk up and join Pam on stage. "Ladies and gentlemen; this wonderful man is my newlywed husband Joe, and these are our wonderful children; Andromeda Christina and Leonidas Timothy...Hampton." The reporters applaud as Pam notices Gia Christakis' eye bulge out. "And to answer the seriously funny expression on Gia's face down here, our children chose these hair-styles."

And Channel 8's Gia Christakis smiles. "My question is for Andromeda and Leonidas. What gave you the crazy idea to cut all your hair off?"

Nineteen

Romy stands next to Pam and someone hands her a wireless mic to answer Gia's question. "Ms. Christakis; when our new mom found us, we had dirty clothes, faces, bodies, shoes and a bad case of head lice." Gia makes a face which tells Romy that's a rough situation. "We lucked out since a member of Mom's family has a Health Dept. waiver to give haircuts to clean up rough stuff. So, I asked if my hair-style could resemble Demi Moore's from *G.I. Jane*. Leo just likes having his head shaved."

The press laughs as Romy hands the mic to the person who handed it to her. Then a woman of fine Latina stature holds her mic up as Channel 6's Liz Herrera asks Pam, "Captain Hampton, given the arrest of Det. Constantine and the fact he was related to you; how would you rate your effectiveness as the current command officer of the Major Case Squad?"

Pam carefully considers the question. "One case or person related to one case; does not give enough credence to rate one's job performance one way or another Liz. You have to lump together all the casework of a cop or command officer to judge accurately his or her effectiveness. And on the note, you just made; it's a highly speculative and extremely prejudicial question I refuse to answer based on someone's slant in the press."

Jennifer steps up, "Thank you ladies and gentlemen; that's all for today." The press clamors for more as we escort Pam, Thea, and the rest of the family away from the conference room.

Pam stops and put her hands on her face and wipes back and slicks her hair back. "What the hell was I thinking answering that impossible question?"

"You answered it the best way possible given how she phrased the question," Jennifer shakes her head.

"Normally, Liz does a better job at researching scenarios before she asks questions like that; I wonder what happened?"

Pam shakes her own head and smiles at Jennifer. "You remember that press conference when she questioned our professional integrity when trying to protect Kat due to the Russian Mob and FSB chasing her?" Jennifer smiles and nods. "She made my response sound, not only unprofessional, but corrupt. And instead of using bad judgment and slugging her in the jaw like I wanted to do, you talked me down and I turned and responded, 'I will not dignify that question with an answer Ms. Herrera. Which begs whether you can conduct yourself in a professional manner or not Ms. Herrera?' And I turned and walked away."

Jennifer smiles. "If I remember correctly, she wasn't too thrilled about that answer. And for that matter, Mayor Reyes was less than thrilled about your response either."

"At this point, both cases are over, and the Russians look more corrupt than we do. Although as a country, we probably run a close second or third in the minds of some in the world," Pam sighs as she hugs Romy and Leo. "Not the welcome home I was hoping for, but I'm glad you guys are here."

Then someone walks in uninvited; Channel 6's Liz Herrera steps up and hands Pam a document, "What the hell is this Liz?"

"It's an injunction barring your adoption of these children according to State Adoption Laws in Texas. CPS workers are waiting outside to take the children to a foster home."

Pam risks coming unglued on Herrera as Jennifer hands the legal document to Thea and Mike. "What's the allegation prompting this document Ms. Herrera?" Thea asks pointedly as she reads it over. "Channel 6 alleges they discovered living, more suitable family members for the children. So, where are they?"

Liz smiles like an evil witch. "We're not at liberty to say."

"Then CPS will produce those names prior to our release of the children to their custody, or we will return them to Mrs. Martinez in Chicago until custody of the children, is properly sorted out."

Pam said as Jennifer steps up and nods. "Because Ms. Herrera, since the adoption took place in Chicago, a neutral party will accompany the children back to Chicago until this matter is settled...as per U.S. Adoption Laws governing all fifty states of the United States; Ms. Herrera."

"Actually, I want to sue Channel 6 for custodial interference!" Everyone turns in shock to see Romy's arms crossed and angry eyes. "As well as the State of Texas."

Liz Herrera looks into Romy's angry eyes. "You can't be serious!"

"Actually Liz; she is serious!" I say as I present the adoption paperwork for us, by the children, to adopt us as their parents. "According to this paperwork, Andromeda, and Leonidas Drivas, adopted Pam and I as their parents of record; hence legally changing their names to Hampton. So, yes; she's deadly serious."

"In fact, Chief Vaughn; is there still a strong contingent of the press available for Romy to address Channel 6's and CPS' concerns about the adoption?" Thea asks since she's an attorney and can assist in addressing the legal ramifications of the adoption process.

Jennifer looks over to her Officer in Charge of Public Information; Lt. Linda Spears. "I'll call them back and Miss Hampton will be allowed to give a statement to the press concerning her adoption."

Liz Herrera almost burst a blood vessel, "You're actually going to make a statement about your adoption and then sue my station and the State of Texas? Who do you think you are young lady?"

Before Romy answers, Pam whispers in her ear. Then she answers Liz, "I am a US citizen exercising my First Amendment rights to be heard by the press. You are not allowed to legally prevent me from being heard unless you are corrupt in your own right." Romy continues the stare-down with her mature opponent Liz Herrera. She looks over to Lt. Spears, who gives her a *thumbs up!* She smiles like a satisfied imp. "Let's meet the press!"

"Wait!" Liz yells as she takes the injunction and tears it up. "I did that as a ploy, because I wanted to interview the children."

Romy walks up with Pam standing by her side and utters in a clear voice, "If you're going to treat my mother with such...disrespect; I wouldn't grant you an interview if you were the last reporter on earth!" She looks into Pam's smiling face, "Our public awaits?"

"They do; you ready to face them now Miss Hampton?" Pam smiles at our beautiful, brave daughter.

"Yes, Captain Hampton," Romy smiles as she looks at Liz Herrera. "Outta my way Toots; I have public to address!" Everyone chuckles as an indignant Liz Herrera stands aside for my daughter–Andromeda Christina Hampton.

"Nice job on that statement kiddo," I smile as I hug Romy.

"Thanks Dad," Romy hugs me back as my parents arrive. Mom and Dad walk up with big smiles on their faces as Pam and Leo join us. "Well, these are your parents Dad? It's nice to finally meet you in person...Grandpa and Grandma!"

"Same here!" Leo smiles as he gives Dad a bear hug.

"Ah now that's a manly hug from a ten year old young man!" Dad laughs as he releases Leo's embrace. "He hugs like John did when John was ten."

Mom smiles as she gets her share of hugs and kisses from Romy and Leo. "This is how to meet grandchildren; hugs and kisses all around." Mom's joy is subtle; which means she's made some calls to Austin considering the nature of the adoption. And I see the look in her eyes; her news isn't good. "I called a friend in Austin who works for Child Protective Services. Illinois' office set an unusual, legal precedent allowing Romy and Leo to adopt you and Pam. In one aspect; it complicates the adoption papers you signed for them. On the other hand, any ACLU attorney worth their salt would see this as an opportunity to challenge the law the way it's written."

Pam adds, "Like children divorcing their parents or becoming emancipated minors; their wishes must be considered legally binding in the eyes of the law. I'm glad I'm related to a lawyer and she's married to one." Pam eyeballs Thea and Mike; who both smile and nod. Something tells me we're about to have some serious fun with the legal system.

Two hours later, A-USA Antonia Melendez, Nueces County Asst. Dist. Attn. Kyle Madison, and Mike as well as Thea; meet to discuss not only our mutual adoption with Romy and Leo, but the human-trafficking case against Cyrus and Margie Williams. Toni, as A-USA Melendez is known in some circles, speaks as to the progress of that case. "Kyle and I spoke with the A-USA working with the FBI Violent Crimes Task Force in Chicago. The Williams' caused quite a stir after being indicted on human trafficking charges. And based on Romy and Leo's statements, the FBI mobilized offices in Fayetteville, St. Louis, Springfield, and Chicago. They found sixteen dead children along the way; part of the group Romy and Leo suspected of disappearing."

Thea asks as Pam and I are present due to Pam's work in Chicago, "What about the members of the Drivas family; allegedly killed by Cyrus Williams' cult?"

Kyle's demeanor matches his light blue suit with a vest and red tie. "The FBI found those bodies and evidence connecting the cult to them."

"And another bit of good news; when CPS here discovered Romy and Leo were under a material witness order for this case, prior to their adoption case, CPS decided not to pursue placing them elsewhere. But Joe, Pam; there will be home visits and a home study in six months. So be warned, they will be checking."

"Was this a request by each state that signed off on this process; or by Channel 6 News because they disrespected everyone connected to this case?" If Pam had not asked, I would've asked. Apparently, Cyrus Williams fears what will be said at the trial.

Kyle fields that question, "Channel 6 did play a part due to the denial of an interview by Romy. But on the same note, Gia Christakis of Channel 8 championed your cause due to Sir Geoffrey's status with the Kasumatis family in London as well as the main family in the Aegean. Liz Herrera learned there are enough positive Greek influences for Romy and Leo to develop a proper, cultural identity."

"Speaking of which," yes, I have to chime in since Kyle mentions the phrase *proper cultural identity*. "Anyone address why Cyrus and Margie tried to change Romy and Leo's legal first names? It sounded as if they tried to wipe the children's cultural identity from their birth records."

Toni smiles; I love it when an A-USA smiles like that. "We informed CPS of these issues as well as the accusations of abuse made by the children against the Williams couple. We also saw the *before* pictures when you first met them and the *after* pictures. Mrs. Carmichael at CPS felt the haircuts were extreme, until she learned later the children chose those hair-styles. Then during her interview, Romy asked Mrs. Carmichael why she felt she was qualified to decide where she and Leo would live?" I watch as Toni shakes her head and laughs. "But Pam gave her strong encouragement to behave and let Mrs. Carmichael finish the interview. Mrs. Carmichael informed us that was a point in your favor as to your positive influence. Leo's interview was pretty much trouble-free; but you needed to be present because he does have trust issues with adults he doesn't know. And again, another point in your favor."

"But a lack of blood relation...subtracts several points away from us," Pam notes to Toni's sad nod. "What else do we have to face in this uphill battle?"

Toni shakes her head; apparently some wild card no one anticipates appears to rein havoc on our attempts of having a family. "The attorney for CPS went to Huntsville to interview disbarred attorney Miles Covington. The plan is to enter his affidavit as evidence you are unfit to be a mother."

"Who is the attorney representing CPS in this matter?" Pam asks and the response chills her to the bone when she reads the case file. "Anita Matthews-Wells; of Wells Gardelli of Dallas, Texas." Pam sheds bitter tears as she leaves the room.

I follow her and hold her. "We will deal with this babe."

"Tell me Joe; how in the hell do we deal with Dr. David Matthews's ex-wife? She's Flora's partner and has no clue what's happened in the last three months!" Then the raven-haired ex-wife attorney of David Matthews walks up. "Why are you doing this?"

"It's the law Pam!" Annie Wells yells in response. "It is always advantageous to have a biological attachment to the children concerned. Yes, they trafficked them, and yes; they were in a pitiful condition; but they are still related to them by blood! I'm sorry, but that's the law!"

"I'll remember that; the next time one of...your kind...needs a stake pulled out of their sides when someone tries to dust you," Pam speaks low enough to where only Annie can hear her. "I'll simply let the next immortal take you out." Annie realizes she just lost a friend, and the respect of someone she owed her life. "And Jennifer; she sends her regards as well; Counselor!"

As we walk out of the building and join Jason, Jennifer, all the kids, as well as Thea and Mike; I look to Pam. "Tell me that was a Marine Corps-like threat you just made?"

Pam whispers to me, "Damn straight it was Longhorn!" I smile.

Twenty

During the prep for the human-trafficking case against the Williams' and the Lord's Light Brigade Church, CPS forced us to allow supervised visits with the Williams family. However, the children keep their distance from Cyrus and Margie. "Well, the children look good for the shape they were found I assume," Cyrus smiles as Romy stays right under Pam's left arm. "Come over here Andrea, give Papa a kiss please?"

Annie Wells lets into her client. I believe she realizes Pam's concerns weren't just insane ramblings. "Mr. Williams, do you find it difficult to call your granddaughter by her given name? According to her legal birth certificate, it's Andromeda. And your grandson's legal first name is Leonidas. We discussed this at your bail hearing and arranged the case to be tried here in Corpus Christi. What are you afraid of Mr. Williams?"

"Their names were changed legally to reflect their proper status as Americans! Those...foreign names are a poor reflection of how this country has lost its way! Andromeda, Leonidas; what kind of names are those for my grandchildren?" Cyrus rushes forward. "You will come here now, or I'll whip you girl!"

We all restrain Annie and Margie as Cyrus rushes the children. Leo performs a front leg sweep and knocks Cyrus off his feet and Romy grabs the old man's neck and his face stares in horror up into mine. "Mrs. Wells, this is an example of the discipline and the family bonding we've done with Andromeda and Leonidas since their adoption has been challenged. Due to Mr. Williams' so-called outburst; the children felt the need to protect themselves from such rants. And as you can see, they performed the self-defense strategies with...lethal precision; if necessary." I look over at a stunned and horrified Mrs. Carmichael.

A Nubian goddess of refinement and articulation in her pink skirt suit with white blouse and matching pumps. "Mrs. Carmichael, is it still the State of Texas' opinion that the children be returned to their maternal grandparents?"

Mrs. Carmichael looks to me and then to Pam. "How do I know you two are any better for them; given their behavior towards Mr. Williams?" Now this is a funny situation: a CPS worker, judging the behavior of children trafficked against their will, rescued, and taught survival tactics; and used against a violent and unstable grandparent. Obviously, Mrs. Carmichael's opinion of cops and private eyes is slightly prejudiced against.

I answer her query, "The violent tendencies of this grandparent I'd call into question. And as stated, my children defended themselves."

Pam smiles and looks to Romy, "Kiss and makeup Romy; then come over here to me please?" Romy kisses Cyrus on the forehead while still holding his neck in a position to break it. She quickly lets go and runs over to Pam's protective embrace. Leo walks over and hides behind me. "Something missing in the parenting style of the maternal grandparents is mercy and love. They wish to win souls to the Lord; same as the Greek Orthodox Church, but without love and mercy from Almighty God; their faith is worthless. Mrs. Carmichael, I requested background on you at CPS regarding your personal life. And I am impressed in addition to trying to do the best for the children you place, you also teach Sunday school to fourth graders."

"So, you found out some information about me; what's that prove?" Mrs. Carmichael makes a valid point with her question. What does it prove?

Then FBI Special Agent Cass Coltrane of TFCC walks into the house. "I can answer your question Robby; provided you're willing to listen...to a federal cop?" Carmichael nods as Cass hands her a tablet.

Cass starts with one video file and Carmichael observes several situations where we taught and disciplined both kids at different times. She also observed us...teaching them examples of grace, love, and mercy within our family. "During the last forty-eight hours, we were asked to observe this family as part of the prep for both; the custody hearing and the pre-trial events of the human-trafficking case. The most recent...bad behavior of Mr. Williams, will be forwarded to the US Attorney's office here in Corpus Christi. We didn't do this to help either the Williams' or the Hamptons; we did this to protect the safety and welfare of two, underage, material witnesses in a federal case."

"I see," Carmichael looks to Romy and Leo. "What you did a moment ago, I don't approve. However, given the accurate fact; I am making judgments without reviewing this case on both sides, your actions to defend yourselves...I agree must be allowed. I will make this suggestion: let your guardians handle that before you two dive in like that please?"

"Yes ma'am," the kids respond in stereo.

"And we have discussed the issues of certain inappropriate behaviors which will not be tolerated in this household; haven't we Romy?" Pam asks pointedly.

"Yes ma'am," Romy quietly responds as she walks up and hugs Pam. "And to you Mrs. Carmichael, I apologize if what I said yesterday in anyway sounded...disrespectful. That question was not about your ability to do your job. I questioned your desire to put Leo and I in a situation you knew wasn't safe." Romy looks to Pam and shakes her head. "And if someone in your department forces this reunion; I will be forced, respectfully, to file a custodial interference civil suit against CPS and the State of Texas...ma'am."

Robby Carmichael gives Pam and Romy a leery glance. "Is she serious Capt. Hampton?"

"I wish none of this had happened," Pam sighs, "However, we spoke with Mrs. Martinez at the Chicago office of the Illinois CPS office.

"The Illinois Atty. Gen. is upholding the legal decision for Romy and Leo's adoption of Joe and I as their parents. So unless you plan on challenging the State of Illinois' legal decision, Romy and Leo have grounds for a class-action lawsuit against the State of Texas."

Robby Carmichael shakes her head at Romy and Leo. "You really believe this cop and private eye serve your best interests and those of your brother young lady?" Romy nods and Leo nods with her. Mrs. Carmichael's confidence still leaves little to be desired as Thea steps up. "And you are?"

She presents her newest business card. "Athena Flynn–Attorney at Law. The firm of Flynn/Papadakis has been retained by the Drivas children and duly appointed as their advocates by both the State of Texas and of Illinois. Any attempt to remove them from this home prior to the human trafficking case's decision, will be met with a legal quagmire even Bill Clinton wouldn't want to face." Then Cass hands a document to Thea, who scans it over and smiles. "This is the material witness order signed by the FBI in Illinois and now signed by the FBI Assistant Director in Atlanta, GA. I don't care for your less than professional attitude toward Mr. or Captain Hampton. And any, and I mean, any further less than professional attitude from your standpoint, and I will request a replacement case worker for my clients. Also, these notations as well as the Williams' outbursts will be factored into the case. I can promise you that Mrs. Carmichael." Mrs. Carmichael huffs a response and leaves. Then Thea walks up and stands nose-to-nose with Annie Wells. "We have fulfilled the terms of the supervised visit Mrs. Wells. However, your client, Mr. Williams, attempted to assault my younger clients. As such, under the terms of supervised visitation for the children, I have to recommend the courts suspend all visitation by the Williams' and their family members until a decision in the human trafficking case, is rendered." Annie looks back at her clients, faces Thea, and nods.

"When do you plan to file the motion?"

Thea looks at her clients and then to Cyrus and Margie. "I plan on filing the motion tomorrow morning in Family Court."

Annie nods as she looks to Pam's angry glare. "You were right Captain Hampton; the Williams' are not a safe option for Romy and Leo. I will inform the Family Court office of that fact when I withdraw as counsel for the Williams family."

"This is outrageous!" Cyrus yells as he rushes forward again. This time, Annie stiff-arms him, and he falls backward into a chair. "How in God's name did you do that?"

"Advanced martial arts training," Annie smiles as she looks back to me and Pam and winks. "Captain and Mr. Hampton, would you and Agent Coltrane escort the children, and the Flynns into the family room please? The Vaughns and I...need a private word with my former clients." I smile as we nod and take the kids into the family room with Cass. Hopefully, Annie will use that magical voice she learned from her ex-husband to make them confess their sins; preventing them from ever getting Romy and Leo.

While I play chess with Romy with Leo watching, Cass smiles at Pam and gives her some comfort concerning our Arkansas interlopers. "The um...conversation she's about to have, will not be recorded due to a maintenance pulse signal being sent right about...now."

"Why now Cass my love?"

"The little voice Annie utilizes in this instance might cause a little...problem if a recording exists; hence we arranged the maintenance pulse in the surveillance system to coincide with that little discussion." Pam shakes her head as if Cass has to explain how...hypnotic that particular voice can be. The reason Annie called the Williams couple down, is she felt...guilty about how you two left things the other day."

"Which part: where I ripped her stuff about the kids' safety, or the fact I'd not help out like I did before?" Pam's response is measured, but thoughtful.

Cass smiles as she watches Leo break off and draw a picture in pencil.

"Well that last part did sort of motivate her to rethink sometimes...the legal thing to do isn't always the right thing to do." Pam laughs as Annie walks into the family room. "What's with the big smile legal eagle?"

Annie's grin radiates the room. "The Williams' have waved legal representation and have decided to confess to all and allocute in open court; preventing the necessity for the human trafficking case to go to trial."

"Meaning...what exactly?" Pam's question does have merit.

"Meaning I should've listened to my better angels and upheld the spirit of the law equally as the letter of the law," Annie smiles sadly. "Also, I thought like a grandparent since I became one in the last three years. I forgot, people who can love children like you and Joe; need that opportunity. I'm sorry I stepped in the middle of it."

I could see the sorrow in Annie's eyes and so could Pam. There are times my wife's heart just breaks for some hard luck cases. Then again, if my ex-husband's wife lost favor with the international financial community of late, I'd probably be a little uncertain as to my future in my chosen profession. So Pam demonstrates to Romy and Leo something she feared she couldn't do...forgive Annie Matthews-Wells. "You were doing your job Annie; I can't fault you for that."

"I know, but I fault me; believing some cult leader would change to try and be good guardians for their grandchildren. But I have to remember: these people killed their own daughter. How safe are they for the children?"

"Ms. Annie; Leo and I forgive you," Romy says as she walks up and hugs the dark-haired attorney. "We were told what the law about adoptions said; it's hard to trust when you've been treated so badly. But when we met Joe and Pam; something told us we could trust them. Then when they took us to get cleaned up, fed us, and got us nice clothes; we knew they cared about us. If you were us Ms. Annie, who would you trust?"

I could see Annie smile and shake her head from side to side. "Having been in a close-to-similar circumstance, I'd trust the ones who chose to care and love me for me; not some fake version of me." Then Annie looks to Pam again. "Anyway Jen will ever trust David or Nikki again?"

Pam sighs heavily; the subject's still touchy even after three months passing. "I can't answer that Annie. I know Ben Kowalski's family, Mark Devlin's family and Michael Cruz's family; want both their heads on a pike. CCPD's closed off to them now. Electronic dampening fields, atmospheric monitoring, and other natural countermeasures are in place against David and/or Joshua's...abilities of infiltration. That's why the security systems at CCPD, our homes, and Jason's beach house, all have these countermeasures in place." Annie now understands and has gauged the level of distrust any and all DMD-related personnel have earned. "I don't know if I can, given the fact I was trying to do Jen a favor by looking after Kat and her parents; then the Russians came after us. Annie, my father, in his opinion, had to become a Greek mob boss to protect his family, even me and Thea."

Annie's hand rises over her mouth out of instinct. Now she understands Pam's anger and frustration. "How does that affect you now?"

Pam shakes her head. "Before we left Chicago; Thea and I...disowned our parents and any other family tries to interfere in our lives here. Then I saw something...that scared the hell out of me."

"You mean Jennifer's wolf face?" Annie smiles as Pam's shock registers with Annie; me too. "Yes, the one little *Frankenstein* experiment my ex didn't think would come back and bite him in the butt...and it did when Jen tried to protect Kat and her parents. David synthesized a retrovirus based on Jason's tribal heritage. The side effect: Jason and Jennifer are now connected by spirit and by blood. So now, due to what Jason and Jennifer...have lost; they have an extremely fragile truce with David and Dominique."

I watch as Annie's piercing blue eyes glance my way and nod as I shake my head. "Unfortunately, David and Nikki dug that hole in the beach, and they will have to live with the consequences of their actions or inactions. Dillon's just completed rehab for his gunshot wound and Gracie's still too angry to speak with even Sean and Katie Matthews. Sean rode her pretty hard about protecting her aunt. I'm literally shocked she didn't shoot him she was so angry."

Annie sighs; an indicator she agrees with most of what I just said. Pam further chimes in. "Annie, between those two couples, we have to be Switzerland. I work for Jen and Joe's distantly related to Nikki. Putting us between them is only going to anger us further. And now, I have a possible fledgling family to consider as well."

"All things being equal; who would you want in a firefight, if it came to that?" Annie asks a relevant and unfair question. However, David and Dominique have larger concerns than Pam or I at this point.

So my only answer is just as unfair, but also more meaningful. "I'd have to side with the Vaughns. Yes, I'm distantly related to Nikki. Yes, both the Vaughns and the Stocktons have business dealings with the Matthews Ranch in Abilene. And yes...Jim Vaughn and my uncle Jacob have a Vietnam-era connection with Paul Matthews. But, given the constraints and clan law David must honor first; how often can he exploit or circumvent that law to step in and be involved what is clearly...mortal concerns?"

Annie smiles and nods. "You're right; neither David nor Nikki has considered the long-range consequences of their actions. Jason and Jennifer have their own problems and some of those were caused by my ex and his wife. And as a result, people who should be alive today...are dead. I'll gently remind them as well you have millions of shares in DMD stock you won't hesitate to sell off if you get ticked off by them." I smile my wicked grin and nod. Then Annie looks at our kids. "Yeah, you two will do okay with Joe and Pam." Annie smiles and leaves.

Twenty-One

Saturday, June 18[th,] and we've finally settled into a routine. A week prior, Cyrus and Margie Williams made their confession a matter of public record in regards to the human trafficking charge stemming from the murder of Michael and Annabel Drivas. The former leaders of the Lord's Light Brigade Church; allocuted to the murders of their daughter and son-in-law, 18 children en route to Chicago from Fayetteville, AR, and to illegally selling Romy and Leo to the Krontzky Crime Family.

Two days after the allocution, Romy and Leo testified at the sentencing hearing; in which the judge gave to Cyrus and Margie each, three-consecutive life sentences without the possibility of parole. The judge further ruled that due to the treatment of Romy and Leo by the family, no one related to the Cyrus/Margie Williams family, was eligible to adopt the children. Judge Michaela Strawn, an older red head with considerable time on the bench, further ruled, "According to the agents of Task Force Corpus Christi and the corporate counsel for DMD International, I will be recommending to Family Court that Andromeda Christina Drivas and Leonidas Timothy Drivas, be allowed to remain with Joseph and Pamela Hampton as their children, as well as the aforementioned couple remain their parents."

When Judge Strawn pounded her gavel, Leo leapt into my arms and Romy assaulted Pam with a bear hug. Robby Carmichael walks up and smiles. "I've already been informed by Judge Macon in Family Court; he's upholding the rulings in both Texas and Illinois that the kids have the right to adopt you two as you to adopt them."

"I hear a pronounced *but* in your voice." Yes, I am asking because there is a pronounced *but* looming.

"Mrs. Martinez did agree with me one home visit and a home study be performed to check on the status and welfare of Romy and Leo. At this point, those are simple formalities." Mrs. Carmichael smiles.

"What's required?" Pam ever so vigilant.

"The home study can be with either one of you at home at the time. But we would like to have the home visit with both there and observe how you four are getting along as a family," Mrs. Carmichael says as she consults her appointment book.

Just then Jason and Jennifer walk up and are followed by David and Dominique. Jennifer looks over her shoulder, smiles, and faces us. "I hear the adoption was upheld...congrats you guys." Jennifer hugs Romy and Leo as Jason looks back and smiles at David and Dominique.

"However Chief, Mrs. Carmichael is still obligated to conduct one home visit and a home study to see how we're all getting along." And I have to get my two-cents in since I'm now unofficially a dad. "So Pam and I are waiting to hear what days are convenient with Mrs. Carmichael; primarily to my thinking, she has more than one active case concerning adoption or foster care."

"I can assist with that dilemma some. Pam, take the next two or more weeks. If necessary, come back after July 4th." Jennifer smiles as Pam embraces her. "Mrs. Carmichael, if that helps, can you see a way to deal with those issues as quickly as possible? Because if I'm not mistaken, Captain and Mr. Hampton have a plan as to Romy and Leo's continued education as well as a plan for participating in their local home-school cooperative."

"Seriously now," Mrs. Carmichael smiles her suspicious smile. Then David and Dominique raise their hands. "I take it you two have a hand in this?"

"We...indirectly, have-a-hand in this Madame." Dominique squirms like she did when she was being taught religion by nuns in Greece.

"We informed the courts regarding the murders of the three detectives in the protection of one Katerina Petrov, which we tried to prevent the incidents, but failed in our attempt. The District Attorney offered as part of a plea deal, my husband and I...serve as guest lecturers and also be accredited as teachers at a special co-op facility."

"And what capacity will Dr. Matthews serve?" I could see Robby Carmichael's eyes shimmer with mischief in the question.

"I will serve as a guidance faculty member in the science areas of the curriculum. We will have different levels based on the ages of the children and families involved. And this will include the families of the detectives who lost their lives in the line of duty."

Mrs. Carmichael nods her acknowledgement as she makes a notation. "I believe we can wave the home study...provided I can do the home visit and witness the family interaction for an evening, say the 22nd of June? I hear Ms. Romy's a fantastic cook."

Romy looks to Jason and Jennifer, "Okay which one did it?"

"Did...what Romy?"

"Which one of you told Mrs. Carmichael about my cooking?" Romy watches as Jason playfully hides his face and Jennifer looks around and whistles to no one in particular.

I never said my good friends Jason and Jennifer Vaughn were good actors, but they are good people. And in all my years, I never saw Jason Vaughn crack like my father would under pressure. But on this occasion, the poor man succumbed to Romy's cute smile. "Oh all right I confess, I ratted you out! But only because I wanted to enjoy another round of Lemon chicken or roasted lamb."

"The Apple Milopita with ice cream had nothing to do with the admission to Mrs. Carmichael; did it Agent Vaughn?" Jennifer said as Pam nods with a satisfied smile on her face. Poor Jason, done in by my twelve-year old daughter.

"I hope you ladies realize; I haven't been this accosted by cuteness since Gracie was born.

"And the dessert portion of the menu had nothing to do with my…spontaneous admission to Mrs. Carmichael." Jason shakes his head and takes a breath before he utters another word. Gotta hand it to old *Specter* for trying to keep his cool. "In all my years as a federal agent, I've never been horn-swoggled by anyone, much less a kid."

Romy walks up and flashes her cute grin under Jason's nose. Then to everyone's surprise, Romy kisses Jason on the cheek and walks over to Jennifer. "He's gotten soft in his old age, hasn't he Chief?"

Jennifer looks at the red lip print on Jason's cheek and slowly shakes her head. "Yep, that's my fearless Comanche warrior…soft-hearted with a soft head!"

Just then Gracie walks out to meet us. Jennifer's 'mini-me' stands five feet five inches weighs a pitiful one-hundred pounds soaking wet. Where this girl puts food is any body's guess. Her light brown hair and hazel eyes match Jennifer look for look. The tan tank top with black athletic shorts denotes her relaxed look for a star athlete from Mary Carroll High School here in Corpus Christi. She sees Pam and walks over to hug her. "Hi Aunt Pam; I see you made it back from Chicago in one piece. Hey Uncle Joe!" When she sees David and Dominique, her scowl intensifies. "Mom, is everything okay?"

"It's all right babe; Uncle David and Aunt Nikki were just leaving." David and Dominique look over at Gracie and see her eyes glaring howitzer holes through them. "And the twins will be forwarding their apologies soon I understand?" Jennifer turns to glare at the Matthews couple as well. "Right?"

"Yes, those apologies will be written and forwarded as soon as possible." Dominique hides her face from Gracie's angry stare.

Gracie holds up her hand and shakes her head. "Don't bother; I know Sean's and Katie's minds. Katie would genuinely be apologetic about the matter. Sean, he's still mad because I have a boyfriend and it's not him. I'd rather it be a genuine apology from both instead of a forced one from either."

David and Dominique simply nod and leave. Gracie turns and faces Jennifer. "I'm sorry; I'm not at the point where I can forgive or be nice to them for pity's sake." Then she leans in thinking no one else can hear. "Plus, Aunt Flow's visiting."

"My least favorite aunt as well," Pam smiles as she hugs a half-smiling Gracie. Then Romy and Leo walk up to the wiry teenage Gracie. Gracie notices the hair styles and gives Pam a *what did you do to these poor waifs* look. Pam smiles. "Gracie, these are our new family members: Andromeda and Leonidas Drivas...now Hampton. Romy, Leo; this is Aunt Jennifer's daughter Gracie."

Romy sticks out her hand. "Pleased to meet you Gracie. Mom?" Romy looks to Pam whose smile beams at the title of *Mom*. "Since we're fixing a full course meal, would it be okay for the Vaughns to join us?"

"I don't see why they can't; if so, we need to inventory the menu for that night to make sure we're feeding an army as well," Pam looks over at Thea and nods. "I mean, we're not only having our family, Mrs. Carmichael and the Vaughns over; but Uncle Mike, Aunt Thea and Sean as well as Liam." Gracie gives Pam a confused look as Thea's family steps forward. "Sorry Gracie, this is my sister Athena, my brother-in-law Mike and their two boys, Liam and Sean. Liam's the oldest."

"Welcome to Corpus Christi," Gracie smiles as Liam and Sean shake her hand in turn. "Be careful Mrs. Flynn, your boys might end up breaking a lot of hearts down here."

"Hearts...Mom?" Sean asks. Clearly, Gracie's purpose to start a little troublesome controversy's about to backfire. I see Thea smile and shake her head. "Dad, why is Mom smiling like that?"

Mike saves the day...or does he? "Guys, what Gracie's trying to say is girls might swoon when you get interested in them."

"Girls...yuck!" Liam and Sean's stereo answer make everyone laugh at once. I see Jennifer mouth *Stop that* to Gracie. Leo joins in the current rendition of the *He-man Woman-hater's Club*.

I still love watching those old *Little Rascals* episodes. People always think family and close friends are the best social groups around. I tend to agree, until you have a less than scrupulous aunt try to steal your legacy to line her greedy pocketbook.

"So...Romy...right?" Gracie asks as Romy nods. "You need a Sous Chef for your meal?"

"Sure Gracie; I never turn down help when I'm cooking." Then Romy smiles, "I always like making new friends over a cutting board."

"When cooking, so do I. Other times, I like to bond over basketball or being a mime." When Gracie smiles, Romy's eyes light up with wonder. "What?"

"You mime? I never met anyone younger than an adult who's ever done that! How did you get started?"

"Well, I sort of…fell into it when my mom was in the hospital..." I listen as Gracie tells Romy about her foray into the art of mime. "Like when your birth parents were taken from you, you had to learn to trust others to help you. It's the same as far as coping with a parent being hurt like my mom. Like my dad, my brother wanted to hunt down the guys who hurt her. But when he found out Dad dealt with it legally, Dillon found other ways of coping. He's currently making up classes he missed while he healed. And...he talks with Dad a bunch. It never hurts to pray as well Romy."

Pam looks over at Jennifer and smiles. "It's funny; when you told me about your rape at the hands of those animals, I never thought hearing from Gracie would make me tear-up all over again. But she used it as a transition of how she got into mime. Romy's...listening to her and understanding."

"I tried to tell you long ago; it doesn't take much to bridge understanding Pam." The words drip from Thea's lips like small jars of honey. "You have to be still and listen long enough for understanding to take hold. Too bad Charlie Dupree couldn't figure that out."

"Charlie's problem, both father and son, is their thinking was too ingrained in the culture of the Old South, they forgot the world moved into the 21st Century. And anyone outside of their family was someone to be tamed or subjugated to their way of life." I hear it in Pam's voice; she's moving on past all that hurt and anger the Duprees tried to hang on her. And when it backfired against them; they reacted in the extreme. Thank God she and I are past that nonsense. "I think deep down sometime back, Charlie was in love with me and probably planned on treating me better. But Senior was always an abusive fool."

"Well Captain Hampton, I wouldn't change a thing about our life. I'd even walked the same path on adopting Romy and Leo with you." As soon as I said that, Romy, and Leo pounce on me. "Take it easy you two; I am an old man after all!"

"Aw you're not that old Dad!" I still get all giddy like Pam with all the parental titles floating about. I guess my own father was right; the moment I settle into parenthood, I'd understand how he felt being called 'Dad'. I look to Mrs. Carmichael who simply nods and leaves until Wednesday night.

Twenty-Two

Wednesday arrives in short order as Pam and I gave tours of our offices to the kids. Romy and Leo met members of Pam's Major Case Squad and instantly, recognized Frank Murphy. After a brief conversation on his current status, we adjourned to Pam's office. Romy and Leo marveled at all the awards and decorations; not just from her cop moments, but her days as a Marine. "Mom that flag in the triangle box, with all the medals, what is it?"

"It's called a *shadow box*. The flag of our country is displayed because of my ten year-tenure as a Marine. In front of the flag, are all my medals and awards I received while serving as a Marine. See this medal Romy?" Romy nods as Pam points to a medal with a star and a blue and red ribbon. "That's the Bronze Star; it's given to someone who performs an act of extreme bravery. Mine was I pulled an injured Marine Corps MP behind a barricade after he was shot. Consequently, I also got this beauty. It's called the Purple Heart. That's given to anyone in the Service who gets wounded in battle or in an operational capacity."

"Dare I ask...how you earned the Purple Heart?" Romy's question peeks even Leo's curiosity. And Pam slapped her right butt-cheek. Romy's face winces in sympathy. "Is that why Dad laughed about you getting shot in the butt?"

"I might laugh about it, but since you were shot in Chicago...?" Although Leo's normally fascinated by such stories, Pam's recent foray into her job scares him still.

Pam reaches over and hugs him. "I'm sorry sweetheart. But one day, you'll tell stories to your kids about how your mom the cop, rescued you, Thea, and Romy from some bad people and how...she looked all drugged up in the hospital."

"That might be an interesting story," said a young woman with mocha skin and flashing hazel eyes.

Her navy business suit neatly pressed as Det. Sgt. Sasha Hassan walked into Pam's office. "Welcome back Captain; and I see the rest of the clan's present too. Hi Joe!"

"Hey Sasha, meet our children: Romy and Leo. Guys, this is Det. Sgt. Sasha Hassan. She's been in charge of this unit while your mom and I were in Chicago."

"Pleased to meet you Romy; Leo," Sasha smiles as the kids hug her. When Romy stops hugging, Leo keeps hugging Sasha. "Uh-oh Mom, I think I've gained an admirer."

"That makes how many handsome admirers under the age of 18?" Leo looks up into Sasha's devilish smile and steps back by me. "Sorry about that Sasha. I know how important a love life is to you."

"Oh well, I'll find the right guy one of these days Pam. Anyway, Aunt Jen told me you were coming by for a visit to the squad and bringing the kids along." I help distract the kids as Sasha and Pam continue. "FBI kicked your cousin back to us. TFCC is waiting in Observation and...Aunt Jen's invited you to attend the interview."

After Pam and I drop the kids off with Jennifer in her office, we go down to the interview area and attend the interrogation of former Chicago Det. James Constantine. Before we left, the kids marveled at how much bigger Jennifer's office was compared to Pam's. Something tells me if our kids decide on careers in law enforcement, one will shoot for Jennifer's office.

We arrive in Observation as TFCC agent Boop Garcia and TFCC agent Cass Coltrane interview Constantine. *"So, former Det. Constantine; why did you travel here from Chicago? And don't tell us it's because you wanted to go deep-sea fishing."*

Boop usually filters through all the nonsense so a subject being interrogated; realizes his or her options are limited. Jimmy, as his family knows him, looks into Boop's eyes; trying to deter her game. *"I've already made a statement...Agent Garcia is it? I attended Pam's wedding back in February.*

"You didn't seem like much for an Italian broad."

When Pam and I see Boop's wicked grin, we realize Jimmy just messed up. *"Well Jimmy, you're not the finest example of Greek manliness; more like Greek stooge!"* The moment Jimmy Constantine tries to rise from his seat, Cass sits him back down forcefully. *"You need to be careful Jimmy. You upset poor Agent Coltrane and she's liable to push you down a drainpipe...a very skinny drainpipe. Now, I'm only going to ask this one more time; why are you here in Texas?"*

"I came here to take out that Ruskie bitch, and her family. If necessary, the Vaughn family and even my own if they get in the way! And I was allowed to hunt you people as well!"

I see Cass grab Jimmy under his chin. *"Who told you to hunt us?"*

"Lawyer!"

Jennifer walks in as Pam notices her presence. "The kids?"

"With Sasha in your office. The kids are taking turns playing 'Interim Captain'. Did that idiot cousin of yours just lawyer up?"

"He did." Then Pam gives Jennifer an evil grin. "You know Chief; he's as idiotic as his older brother Angelo. Maybe he needs to speak to the primary targets of the Greek Mob boss's wrath!"

"Then we will need to be...properly disarmed Captain Hampton; as per standard operating procedure." Jennifer smiles as Jason calls the ladies in the room.

We watch as Jennifer and Pam enter the room. Jennifer smiles, *"Our turn ladies and; would you confiscate these items for us please?"* We watch and Jimmy does too, as Pam and Jennifer disarm themselves. Jimmy's eyes widen as each lady removes: a service weapon, a backup on their right ankles; for Pam, a lock-blade knife, and her telescope baton.

Jennifer removes her second back-up Walther PPK from a thigh holster on her left leg and a switch-blade knife from a small sheath on her right thigh. Boop and Cass eye them both wondering if my wife and her boss miss anything.

Pam smiles, *"I believe you ladies have everything now. We'll take it from here."*

"Are you two sure about this? He hasn't been exactly, cooperative." Even though Cass points out the obvious; she's missing the point on why Jennifer and Pam are in there.

Boop, however, sees the light. *"Oh they'll be okay Agent Coltrane. I mean, what could possibly happen to Mr. Constantine since they appear to be unarmed?"*

"You're absolutely correct Agent Garcia. And since this is Chief Vaughn's turf; who am I to upset her plans? Ladies, he's all yours. And Jimmy...enjoy hell!"

Boop and Cass walk out of the room and into Observation. I smile at them. "You two have fun disarming Captain Hampton and Chief Vaughn?"

"We did; what the hell was that all about?" Cass turns to Jason. "Jace?"

Boop smiles. "Think about it girlfriend; he's been cooling his heels ever since he tried to mess with Dillon at TAMU-Corpus Christi. And you see based on the bruising, just how much trouble he's in at the moment? That entire weapon inventory was to lull Jimmy into a false sense of security. We forgot one in the room." When Boop points to Pam, Cass nods in understanding.

"I always forget that part about Marines and SEALs being weapons themselves. Guess I wasn't kidding when I told Jimmy to enjoy hell."

Jason smiles as he watches the room. "Now, the real fun begins."

Jennifer looks to Pam and pulls out a quarter. *"Call it!"* Once when Jason and I taught interrogation techniques at the Iraqi Police Academy, we demonstrated this concept of who got to play *good* cop versus *bad* cop. One would pull out a coin and the other called the flip. The winner played *good* cop and sat down with the subject. The partner stood and played *bad* cop. But unknown to Jimmy, both were about to play a different game; *angry* cop and *psycho* cop.

"Heads!" Pam calls the toss and it lands on the table...tail-side up. *"Oh I was hoping that would happen!"* Pam flashes her best psychotic grin as Jennifer sat down.

Jimmy laughs, *"You lost the toss; I know how that game is played. She's the good cop; aren't you Chief?"* Jennifer smiles and both laugh like a pair of hyenas hunting lions. *"Why you laughing at me?"*

"I find it hilarious that he has no clue how I run an interrogation; does he Captain Hampton?"

Pam shakes her head as she continues to laugh. *"Oh Chief; he has no idea. No Jimmy, this is not* good *cop and* bad *cop; this is* pissed off *Chief versus* Psycho *Constantine/Papadakis cop. Guess which one is which...Jimmy?"* Pam smiles as Jimmy begins to whimper.

"And just so we're clear, Mr. Constantine; we weren't totally disarmed when your cousin and I walked in here. You see, once you've been trained to be a weapon, every other hand-held weapon is an extension of said...human weapon." Jennifer looks up as Pam glares down into Jimmy's face. *"In fact, since this now boils down to an...inner-family squabble as it were; I'll just go get a cup of coffee and let you two sort this out."*

Jennifer rises to leave as Jimmy yells, *"Gustav Papadakis is the Greek Godfather, but he didn't give me my orders!"*

Jennifer sat back down. *"Talk fast; my patience runs thin Jimmy!"*

"It was Thea Maria; she-she gave the orders and had the Russian Mob bosses whacked. I carried those orders out, I'll admit to that, but Uncle Gus didn't give such orders."

Jennifer smiled as she looked to the rest of us in Observation. Then she looked back to Jimmy Constantine. *"And you will...allocute to this in open court?"*

Then Jimmy laughs, we forgot about his attorney. *"You did all this without my lawyer present so; I will not tell all in court!"*

Then Pam leans in and glares at Jimmy. *"No problem Jimmy, I'll send word to the FBI in Chicago that you said who gave the orders to come after my family. And when that knowledge hits the streets, your life as you know, will end violently! So now we will test your loyalties: I call them, and they put the word out you made a deal. Have fun with what's left of your life!"*

"You wouldn't?" Pam nods as she leaves.

She enters Observation. "Let's see how long it takes for him to start waving the lawyer."

Cass smiles sadistically, "Oh Pammy Pam; you're a bad, bad girl!"

"Well you know me Mama Cass; when I'm good I'm good. But when I'm bad, I am so much better!" We all smile as we watch without sound as Jimmy Constantine begins to yell and scream to get an agent or cop into the interview room. A detective with raven locks and lovely brown eyes walks in and calms Constantine down. "That's my newest detective, Sgt. Santana Garvin. She transferred in from the DEA. Santana just finished up with cleaning up a blown Interpol operation in Malta."

Jason nods. "NCIS has an agent who has taken a 60-day voluntary sabbatical. Poor kid's only been with us for a year. Her last six months has been as Agent Afloat aboard the *Ronald Reagan*. She was held prisoner on Malta while the Sicilian Mob sent a stinger into the Command-in-Control deck of the *Abraham Lincoln*."

Jennifer gasps, "Jason, isn't that the carrier...Dewey...?"

Jason nods. "I'm sorry Jen; Dewey didn't make it." Dewey refers to NCIS Agent Afloat Dumont Talbot of Savannah, Georgia. Dewey's cousin was CCPD Asst. Chief of Detectives Grady Talbot.

I watch as Jennifer embraced Jason. She asks, "Did someone inform Grady and Kate?"

"Before Mark, Casey, and Lena left to look into the Honest Abe's situation, Leo called Mark and told him to inform Grady. They left me out of the process due to Kat's situation."

"Grady met with me after Chief-Stat Monday. I told him with Kat's issues; that's why you didn't tell him yourself about Dewey. He understood; didn't like it but understood." I met Grady and Kate and know them to be good people. She's still pregnant and started to show last month. They still don't know whether it's a boy or a girl but hoping for a boy.

Jennifer turns on the intercom and found Jimmy waving his attorney privilege and singing like a bird. *"Yeah, get a U.S. Attorney in here now! I want to talk!"*

Pam watches as A-USA Antonia Melendez walks into the interview room with an attorney waiver and Jimmy signs it as fast as she lays it down in front of him. Then he writes out his statement on his level of participation in the mob boss murders in Chicago as well as all the extra drama by targeting the Vaughn family as well as ours.

Then the U.S. Marshals arrive and arrest James Constantine on conspiracy to murder and other related charges. But due to his testimony, he'll never see the inside of a jail cell. We all walk out as Pam meets her cousin as he's being escorted away. "Toni, could you do me a favor please?"

"Sure thing Pam; what do you want me to do?"

"Tell A-USA Carson in Chicago, to put the word out on the street in Greek Town. Jimmy Constantine flipped on the Greek Godmother. And he's being protected to where no one wants to make a move. And if anyone else gets ambitious enough to do her bidding; I'll return to Chicago, and I'll have legions of loyal followers to raze Greek Town to the ground to clean it up! I will eliminate the Godfather of the Night and anyone who would stand at his side. They want a Cold War; I will give them one colder than the darkest night in Siberia!"

"I will gladly inform A-USA Thomas Carson of that impending. promise Pam. And should he ask, who do I tell him will assist you in keeping that promise?"

Jason smiles and answers, "Tell him Captain Hampton will have volunteers from Hampton Investigations; both offices as well as Task Force Corpus Christi. And anyone else who desires to volunteer to flock to her banner." Toni nods and leaves.

"Oh my god, I'm going to hate writing this report up Jen. Thank God my supervision's been in on this all day long."

"Don't forget your favorite Sorority club Pammy Pam; we've been in on this from this end of the case." Cass smiles, but her smile fades as fast. "And...that's what makes this next part...the hardest. Pam, I'm retiring from the Bureau." Now I understand why Darius and Cass seems so apprehensive, both or just Cass is retiring.

Pam smiles bitterly as she embraces Cass. "I...wish you well my friend."

"You take care of this old girl Corpus Christi, and you watch their sixes until TFCC's full strength again. You hear me?"

"Copy that girlfriend!"

Epilogue

A month passes as Jason comes into my office at the Wells-Fargo Tower over on Upper Broadway. When he wears his navy pin-stripe suit with a white shirt and wine-colored tie, he wants my opinion on a case or a potential agent. In this case, it's a young agent to fill the slot vacated by Darius Coltrane. "So my partner; who's this agent you want me to help evaluate?"

Jason inserts a thumb drive into a slot on my conference table's tablet computer and programs the device to display the image of a lovely young lady with dark brown hair and eyes to match. "Meet Victoria Dominique Blanton of Charlotte, North Carolina. Biological father is Theodore Blanton of Charlotte and mother is the late undercover FBI Agent Charlene Faye Tolliver. I got an old file on the Dixie Mafia from Cass after she retired. Teddy, as his family and friends call him, owns a series of bars and massage parlors in both North as well as South Carolina. Teddy's three eldest children are involved in the business interests of Dixie Mafia Kingpin Joe Don Clayton."

"How?"

"Did Tori evade the mafia life and become a cop? Mama Charlene had a hand in it. And Teddy supported her decision against her older children. I just don't know…how she avoided the life after Charlene and her current husband, Terry Wayne were murdered. All I know, is she finished high school and college before age nineteen. Tori spent time on the pro wrestling Indie Circuit prior to her acceptance at FLETC; then going to DC to train at NCIS under Jerrod Garner."

"After six months with Garner, no wonder she went on Agent Afloat assignment!"

"And during those six months as Agent Afloat, she hooks up with Dewey and works for the SAC out of the Naples office on an Interpol Drug Enforcement case. The Sicilian Mob was tipped off by an FBI agent who wasn't even involved in the case. That agent is being investigated by OPR at the moment." The FBI's Office of Professional Responsibility is called in to look at bad, misguided, or corrupt agents. He's jazzed about hiring Tori. "You're thinking why her for TFCC...Joe?"

"Exactly my question."

"When Tori was sixteen, she lured each of her older siblings, in turn, to her step-grandmother's place in Sneads Ferry, North Carolina. She tied them down to an old medical exam table in a secluded barn on the property and carved a rose tattoo over each of their hearts. Her sister Tessa's was particularly challenging with her boobs."

"Ouch, talk about cutting family ties."

"When SEAL Team Two landed on Malta to rescue the agents still alive from the Interpol op, Tori slowly killed each of her captors and carved similar tattoos on their chests. Scared the mob so shitless; they named her *Rosa del Diavolo*."

"Oh boy, the *Specter* and the *Devil's Rose* under one task force roof; are you sure Washington won't have a shit-fit with what you plan to do Jace?"

"They might Joe; but you have to admit...I can help her where others want to simply toss her aside as damaged goods. Her op was blown, and I can help determine who, what, where, when and why; and I can also make sure the...how; never happens again. I get her to replace Darius, and Santana Garvin as my new CCPD Liaison, I can help her deal with what comes next!"

I smile and nod to my oldest, friend from SEAL Team Three. "Hire her!" Jason nodded.

The Jason Vaughn Case Files
Black Widow Murders
Master Sleuth
Sailor's Blues

Vaughn-NCIS
First Test
Tigers Forever
Law of the Road
Savannah on My Mind
Deadly Force
Operation Night Wolf-Man Hunt
Operation Night Wolf-End Game
The Aunt Boop Mob
The Daughters James
Midtown Strangler

Task Force Corpus Christi
Gulf Coast Wraith
The Panther
Operation Dark Wolf
The Blue Knights'
Little Russian Doll

Joseph Hampton Mysteries
Foreman's Fortune
Suicide Warrior

American Angels
Tag Up
Black Out

Christmas
Savannah Christmas
Christmas I Do's

For more books, go to www.johnsonmedia.biz

About the Author

Growing up in West Texas with only a reading interest in comic books, Jim E. Johnson never cultivated much an interest in reading much less writing. But when TV series such as *Kindred: the Embraced*, and *Buffy the Vampire Slayer*, Johnson looked at writing his first book *Soldier and the Lady*.

After some methodical research led to this first novel published in 2005, he added other writing credits. Which include the novel series lists: *The Jason Vaughn Case Files, Vaughn: NCIS, and the Joseph Hampton Mysteries*. And articles such as: *A Whole New Game* for the Abilene Reporter News, *Market Research Tips and Publishing* for both the Abilene Writers Guild Newsletter and Writing.Com.

Johnson is a former Executive Board Member of the Abilene Writers Guild and a current member of The Authors Marketing International. He lives in Abilene, Texas with his wife Wilma.

www.ingramcontent.com/pod-product-compliance
Lightning Source LLC
Chambersburg PA
CBHW050406070726
47592CB00024B/746